The Way Home and Other Stories

Delores Wade

LMH Publishing Limited

First Edition
10 9 8 7 6 5 4 3 2 1

This is a work of fiction. Names, characters, places and incidents either are the products of the author's imagination or are used fictitiously, and any resemblance to actual persons, living or dead, events or locales, is entirely coincidental.

All LMH Publishing Limited titles are available at special quantity discounts for bulk purchases for sales promotion, premiums, fund-raising, educational or institutional use.

Editor: K. Sean Harris
Cover Design: Roshane Mullings
Book Design, Layout & Typesetting: Roshane Mullings

Published by LMH Publishing Limited
Suite 10-11, Sagicor Industrial Park
7 Norman Road
Kingston C.S.O., Jamaica
Tel.: 876-938-0005; 876-938-0712
Fax: 876-759-8752
Email: lmhbookpublishing@cwjamaica.com
Website: www.lmhpublishing.com

Printed in the U.S.A.

ISBN: 978-976-657-124-5

CATALOGUING-IN-PUBLICATION DATA
AVAILABLE AT THE NATIONAL LIBRARY OF JAMAICA

Name: Wade, Delores, author.
Title: The way home and other stories / Delores Wade.
Description: Kingston, Jamaica : LMH Publishing Limited, 2023.
Identifier: ISBN 9789766571245 (pbk).
Subjects: LCSH: Short stories, Jamaican. | Jamaican fiction.
Classification: DDC 813 -- dc23.

Acknowledgements

Acknowledgements are due to my editor, Ms Lorna Fraser, who read my mind as much as she read my script and provided the glue which has held each of these stories together. I acknowledge persons who stimulated me, from an early age, to appreciate and express my appreciation of people, whatever they are: Teacher Russell, my first head of school held my little hand in his strong hand and led me to the school library held in a cabinet, to select my first story book; my Aunt Ellen who taught me to read; my mother, Daisy who wowed me with her love for anything literary, from excerpts from great speeches to books; my teacher, Edgar Cargill who swung high in his use of English; Ms Nicolson, my teacher of English at Shortwood College who made English a "lived" language; and David Williams, my UWI lecturer/tutor who gave English warmth through literature.

To all who encouraged me to write and meant it, thank you.

Table of Contents

Dying Embers

"What a friend we have in Jesus," Ms Em sang in her tremulous but still beautiful voice. As she crooned, she thought of her younger days when she could 'sing like a bell'. Boy that choir was something — the cantatas, the Christmas pageants, the early morning presentations on First Sunday. She had been in her element then. As she gazed into the flames of the old fireside, her eyes watered and she saw herself: tall, svelte, young, pretty and energetic, going to practices in her lovely, floral, flared skirts, swinging jauntily up the steps and joining the eager group of youngsters, all green with inexperience of the real world.

For them, all was rosy; there was no pain. She sighed in recollection of her contentment then. She recalled more mature years when she sang melodious solos on the choir. She recalled her pleasure at singing in lead roles. She would proudly take her position in the white linen dresses, sometimes the hobbled skirts so tight that she had to step sideways to avoid falling over the high-heeled shoes. Her hair then was soft, black and beautiful, combed back neatly and kept in place by a hairnet under a wide-brimmed hat. The fire needed more wood, she thought, hastily bending to extract some from the pile underneath the fireplace. For a while, her thoughts blurred, and she could not will herself to move.

The smoke from the fire tickled her nostrils, breaking her reverie. Hastily, she fanned the fire into a bright, crackling flame once more. She then busied herself with finishing up breakfast. She inhaled deeply, enjoying the smell of her already golden-brown fried dumplings mingled with the intoxicating smell of the chocolate tea and the sharp, delicious smell of cooked-up saltfish with onions, country pepper and the like. She allowed herself a gentle smile — no one ever refused her dumplings for the fifty years and plenty she had been cooking for people. She surveyed the kitchen fondly: the huge, sturdy fireside with the steel grid resting firmly on the bricks, underneath which lay stacks of firewood; the stand opposite which held lots of gleaming aluminium things on different shelves; bottle after bottle of seasonings and condiments; several quarts of coconut oil so clear you could see through them, and all the other clean clutter of a kitchen well used. She felt a rush of energy overtake her usually tired body.

She went through the routine of taking out a clean tablecloth which she spread on the old kitchen table, blackened by the years. There were always several in the table drawer, ironed and folded, ready for use. She placed the dish and cup on a calico mat that she had lovingly sewn and embroidered some years ago. It carried a picture of a man and a woman holding hands and running across grass so high that their feet were hidden. They seemed to be just running, going nowhere in particular.

She then selected the cutlery she needed from the wooden rack on the kitchen wall, rinsed and dried them, and placed them in position on the table. Not long after, she heard the familiar heavy thud of wood on the ground outside, then the thwack of the axe as he was splitting them. And through the crude board walls of the kitchen, she could hear a rush like the wind accompanying each breath he took as he drove the sharp axe through the pieces of resistant wood. This went on unhurriedly and laboriously for half an hour or so. And she waited, finding little things to do in the kitchen, which had become the centre of her world.

The chopping ended. It was her cue to start the ritual of putting out the breakfast on the table: the large, white mug of steaming chocolate tea, the basin of dumplings and the dish of savoury saltfish. These she covered with an ageing white calico towel, fresh and ironed for the morning. The breakfast provided decoration for the mahogany table blackened with age and always cluttered with stuff she was fond of. Over and over again, he had asked her what she would be doing with all the things there...would she be carrying them to her grave? In a fit of temper one day, he even threatened to dump them.

She always promised to do a spring cleaning...someday she would get around to it, she thought, sighing sadly as she recalled earlier days when she had lived alone or had just married and had been keen on keeping house.

Her own meal was not treated so elaborately. Her one bowl containing everything, alongside her inconspicuous enamel mug, was set casually on the small, narrow table next to the fireside where she normally rested hot pots that could not find a place on the actual grid. She waited, wondering if he would be finished soon. She was really famished now. He had better come now, she thought, or the food would get cold. And then she could not stand the damn argument. After all, she did not have an electric stove. If he wanted his food to be kept warm, he needed to get one. She could almost be sure that he had the money and could do it, but he would not spend that money here. She knew exactly where the money was going, whether it was the pension or the income from the farm.

He came in wiping his hands on the soiled rag he kept in his pocket, in the usual way, as if he were slapping rather than wiping. First the back of his hand, then the front and back again in his own personal rhythm. Promptly seating himself, he glanced at her before starting his breakfast. "Had to go further in the bush this morning."

"Mmm."

"This type o' wood hard to cut and hurt the bad back..."

"We not getting any younger," she remarked, looking at him in a suggestive sort of way. He glanced at her questioningly, deciding to refrain from further comment. This was their way of talking. The ritual had to take place twice daily, and it kept some little thing alive though if you should ask each of the parties what that thing was, each would probably be at a loss for an answer.

He bit purposefully into one of the dumplings, an appreciative breath involuntarily escaping his nostrils. She always cooks so good, he thought. Not having paid her any compliments for a couple of years, he felt a little awkward. She was not expecting any, so his glance of gratitude went unnoticed. She had busied herself with her own meal at the little table, keeping her face turned towards the window for most of the time, an action which allowed her to stare vacantly at her sister's house next door.

This was where she lost herself. She did not need to see anybody. She just needed an object of attention. And the house was just that, a poor, old, board house as was common in that part of the parish, said to be the poorest of the parishes. A strong house it was though, built some forty years ago and surviving without a leak for over thirty years, hurricanes, thunderstorms and strong tremors. It had been home to three children, one of whom had survived the hardest of times and gone to one of the greatest universities in the world. She felt a sudden gush of pride, remembering her help to her sister who had brought up these children. The second was a renowned machinist, and the third, the girl, was very bright but had not had the money to take the examinations of the day. Her eyes grew misty at that. They could not do any more, the two of them. Such is life, she thought, you do not get all you want, but praise God, they were all alive and in good health.

Turning her attention to her husband, she waited, knowing that the next item on the agenda would be the day's activities as told by him: the land he would be ploughing for the teacher; the front lawn he would be cleaning for the postmistress; the bananas he would be cutting for Miss B. All of that with a bad back, she thought, and often without any compensation. But he, old fool, did not seem to mind as long as at Christmas, a bottle of sorrel or a slice of cake could be proudly displayed by him. But the worst part of the situation was how he always made light of the time he spent at Miss B. How casual he tried to sound when he called her name, and yet, he knew that she knew. In fact, everybody in the community knew.

"I coming home early this evening though."

"Okay," she responded, her only emotion shown by a little twist of her mouth.

As early as the other evenings, she thought, with a sardonic smile. So many times he had said that and then reached home late when everything was as cold as a puppy's nose. She kept threatening not to touch any food at those times. He should have eaten where he spent the day.

He had finished eating and was taking the soiled, worn-out crocus bag out from under the table. It was torn in places but the fibres were strong so it could hold up under some strain. Somehow there was always a little hesitation as though he was not quite sure how to transition into the next stage of the day. And so the urgency was carefully camouflaged in little meaningless actions that she was accustomed to. As always, this stage did not last long. He would sit for about two minutes, stretch his long legs beside the table, and look at her as if to ask, "Is there anything you want to say?" Then he would rise from the table with a show of great reluctance, straighten his pants at the waist and making some unintelligible sound, stride carefully outside. She could hear his teeth being brushed noisily on the stand outside. Then he would return to the table where he sat once more to complete his repertoire of actions. Always at this time there was a sense of urgency. He could not maintain his calm any longer; the water boots hastily pulled on, the machete, fork and bag gathered, the hat plunked on his head; and all the time she did not pay direct attention to his motions, now quite routine to her.

"Remember the oil," she reminded him as he hastened through the door.

"I have the bottle."

He was reliable, yes. He took care of all the shopping and paying of the bills between his busy rounds. At least that, she contemplated, seeking anything that looked like compensation. With the old knee bothered constantly by arthritis, she had to depend on him for many of the outside chores. She got up to carry out the rest of the day's work. It was Thursday, so a good pot of red peas soup would be welcome. Pushing her head through the window, she shouted to her sister, Thelma, who came across, greeting her with:

"The man gone."

"Yes m'm."

"Where he said?"

"Oh, all over the district."

"He down bottom yard."

Thelma was now in the kitchen and had taken one of the high square-seated mahogany stools which the rest of the extended family used on various occasions such as when invited for meals. She returned to her seat by the table. The kitchen was their parliament, their confidence chamber, their sports room where they played cards or dominoes after dinner or sat over baskets of stringy, blackie or number eleven mangoes, competitively collected by the four children every day during the mango season. That was a time for reminiscence, a little gossiping about events or people of interest, or soliciting the opinion of the other family members on problems to be solved.

She saw her sister's face fill with concern and anger. She felt her own anger growing, but she fought it away all the way. Shrugging her shoulders, she said with forced casualness:

"You leave young boy alone."

"He young like he son."

"Talk about son. The man writing me to tell me he want to come and spend time."

"You would want him back in you house?"

"No, but the father is here."

"The two of them going to mad you.'

And indeed, it had nearly come to that. He nearly drove his father crazy, and they both drove her almost crazy.

Yes, her life had turned out different from what she expected. Her poor mother had warned her about follow line men. When they were from other villages, they were rightly viewed with suspicion. There were countless stories of how men like those "maltreated" women. She had been too happy to take heed.

"Miss T, the man turn out to be a real old ruffian." She had endured the bad words and the beatings with a sense of resignation.

"But look how you was alright by youself, living in you own little house and taking care of youself."

"True. True. Pity I did not realize and allowed that man to stay."

"You do well, though," said Miss T, shaking her head. "You suffer for over forty years. He so barefaced with the double life. Nearly everything gone to bottom yard. That old witch! What she goin' to tell God? She just living off other women husband."

"But look how long we all in the church. Imagine a woman and a man like that taking communion. In some churches she would get the rod. Sometimes I feel like leaving."

"God communion soon choke some people. Nobody to tell the woman the right thing. Hell will be her portion." Emily was only sorry that she didn't leave when she was younger. No sense in that now. She would soon be gone anyway.

She saw her sister's look of concern and realized she had shut her out for a while. Making light of the moment she offered:

"I want some good peas soup tonight: salt beef, fresh beef, lots of peas."

"Save some for me."

"Of course, I will cook for everybody but I need one of the children to buy the beef."

Miss T took that as her cue to leave and she proceeded with the rest of the day's work. She scraped the fireplace clean of the cold ashes, dumping it at the root of the banana plants immediately behind the house, washed the breakfast dishes and headed for the house, still closed and cold with the early morning air.

Chores completed, she turned her attention to herself, mechanically combing her thinning, grey hair, taking a bath in the little bathroom at the side of the house and returning to the house to lie down for a while. The various tablets she took lay on the press which held all her medicines and personal things. She fetched a glass of water and took out the tablets she needed. She then took a nap.

One day when Miss T thought her sister had completed the morning routine and was resting inside, she went across to her house. But she did not see evidence of the usual tidying up, no broom leaning by the door, no furniture shifted. There was no curtain lifted and no sound inside. And somehow the usual sound of the morning story on the radio did not penetrate the stillness of the house.

Some weeks later, Miss B sat in her living room observing with satisfaction, the tall man sitting across from her. She had fussed over him earlier, giving him a healthy meal of stew peas, which she knew he loved. But half of it was left uneaten on the table. She had talked to him in sympathy, offering her house whenever he needed it, offering her support for as long as he required. He had been polite but throughout their exchange, she had noticed the sadness in his weak eyes. It was not the first time she had seen that faraway look. Yes, he did have some feelings for the wife. You never can trust a man, she thought, her face furrowed with concern. He used to talk as if he hated every bone in her body as well as the bodies of the sister and her irritating grandchildren. She could not believe that after he had casually told her that the old lady was gone, he was now grieving. After all, the funeral had been a whole month ago. Well, it was her time now. She was going to take care of him and get her just reward.

As she walked through the district from day to day, her friends encouraged her to make demands. She was still to stick by him. After all she had always stuck by him. He would be lonely now. She was to make sure he knew that he needed her. It was her time now. Look how long she'd been washing his clothes for a pittance. She was going to be properly paid. All that land they had would belong to her as soon as she got him to make the will.

"B," he said, holding up his head. "I dream the old lady last night and she was looking so sad."

"Sad?" she asked, trying to conceal her scorn. "She should be ashamed of her treatment of you."

"Come to think of it, she was not a bad person. She was a God-fearing woman, and she didn't trouble a soul."

She carefully thought out her response. This was unexpected. He had made commitments to her during Ms Em's life, but all of a sudden, nothing seemed certain. She felt cheated but decided that Emily was not going to rob her in death as well as in life.

"Well, she was you wife, sah."

"She was not a bad wife, fussy but could do a lot of things."

"So, I caa do a lot of things?" With eyelids batting and arms akimbo, she came to stand over him, registering her indignation. "You talk like this woman was a god who couldn' do any wrong. Dats why woman mus'n believe man because they talk through two sides of their mout's."

"Not so I mean. She was good. Grow good and learn to sew, cook, clean and do many things. And she help a lot of people. Even some don't thank her but she really help them."

"I glad you remember those things but mind you get mad, for she gone now. Gone, not to return."

He was not sure that there was any malice in her tone.

"All of us going, B. All of us."

She was nonplussed. She was ready to make plans for taking over the place and hear this man. She walked in deep contemplation to the tank at the side of the house. He was too mixed up for her to ask him to collect the water, she thought. He better sort himself out.

She was not surprised when he said he was leaving.

"You don't want the chocolate tea?"

"No, B," he said, not looking at her. "I going home."

He could not sleep here, and he could not sleep there. Better I dead, he thought. I want my wife with me. How come she just gone like that? I leave her to go do her chores and come back and she just gone.

He turned and twisted but sleep would not come. He got up and went to sit on the verandah. But it was hard because he remembered that at a time like this, she would be sitting at the dining table chewing on something while he sat outside. And then he would come inside and sit at the lamp table, and she would offer him a slice of pudding or cake, or some special fruit drink that had to be had right away so as to prevent spoilage. He missed that. Life would not be the same.

He could not face her grieving family day after day. His eyes brimmed over when he remembered the quarrels and his loss of control. She had a sharp tongue, that woman. She would not take any dirt and he was bad tempered, he knew. Oh God! He needed to talk with his son, soon. He would take the long journey to the district in St. Ann. He wanted to tell him some things about life. He wanted him to tone down that temper and learn to be a good man.

The Way Home

Justine was not comfortable with the tense silence between her and Dirk as they drove out of the city. For her, it was a relief to leave behind the almost unbearable mid-morning heat and the stifling dust of the city. In the magic of the cool, calming country air, her anxiety began to fade, causing the taut muscles of her stomach to gradually become more relaxed. Momentarily, her heartbeat quickened in anticipation of what the day could bring.

But her emotional involvement with nature was unrequited. Her spirits dampened as she watched him drive silently on, seemingly unconscious of the changing atmosphere. His long, dark face set in a grim silhouette, his mouth firm and unsmiling, he spent all his concentration on controlling the almost new SUV over the challenging terrain of the long, winding, uphill road, with its rough, stony surfaces, peeling asphalt and grinning potholes.

As his emotional distance continued, her lightly made-up face began to furrow once more.

But she determinedly fought the stress that started to overtake her body and concentrated instead on what strategy to use to break down the wall between them. She had an almost uncontrollable desire to reach out and touch him, to ask what was going through his mind.

She glanced furtively at him from time to time. Should she push it or should she just go with the tide... shouldn't she be content that she had secured his attention for at least a day... and to think that was a working day for both of them. She fought the negative thoughts of the morning and opted instead to sing one of her favourite songs, 'Every little thing is going be alright'. He always said singing was her worst skill and since she did not want anything to thwart the potential for a happy day, she stopped after one verse but kept the tune going in her mind.

All will be fine, she told herself. Fine? she questioned herself, fine? Yes, she encouraged herself, things will be fine. But, instead of singing, she played the CD with Dirk's own selections. For the first time in ten miles, he reacted, glancing at her in visible relief at the sound of one of his favourite singers.

Nothing could replace her strong desire to talk. This lack caused her spirits to plummet even further and she struggled to maintain a composure she did not feel, something she had been doing for several months.

Her troubled mind wandered to snippets of a private conversation she had overheard in which he had seemed to be reassuring someone about his feelings and intentions.

"You will be patient with me, babe?" he implored.

"Yes, I know it's been long, too long." He seemed to have been interrupted.

"But I have not been idle..."

He said something about being separated by distance.

"But you know I love you, my pet." He sighed. "And I will come through."

She flinched at the seductiveness of his voice, the familiar words he was speaking.

Afterwards, with casual strides, he came into the kitchen and spoke without looking at her as she busily chopped vegetables for the lunch.

"When are you leaving?" he asked.

"You?" she asked, surprised. "Aren't, you coming?" She kept her head down to avoid seeing his eyes or his face.

"Yes, of course," he said, seeming to recollect their plans. "That's what we agreed."

From the corner of her eye, she saw him go back to the dining room where she had laid out breakfast. The clink of cutlery and dishes annoyed her because the scene painted a picture of normalcy. A sudden rage overcame her. It seemed to have emerged from the very pit of her stomach and swelled and strained like an over inflated balloon. She held desperately onto the kitchen counter in an effort to keep herself steady. She breathed deeply, expending her energy in the preparation of the vegetables, the cold chicken slices, sandwiches, the drinks, the fruits and placing everything with purposeful diligence into the various containers, and then packing these into the large wicker basket which they used for outings. At the end of the exercise, she felt easier, as she told herself, her imagination was overactive. That had been her mother's response when, as usual, she shared her suspicions with her at the first sign of something curious happening.

"You are too suspicious, child. Mind you don't cause problems," she had warned as they sat in the restaurant near her office having lunch.

"But Mummy, why is he so late in coming home? Why is he so tardy in getting things done in the house these days? This was not so before," she continued. Her questioning eyes raked her mother's gently wrinkling face as though all the answers she needed were concealed in the caring, light-brown eyes or the soft folds of her cheeks.

"Have you asked him, Justine?" the mother asked, searching her daughter's troubled face. Her own face reflected her concern in spite of the attempt at being casual. She remembered her own story and did not want her child to suffer that experience.

As if not hearing the question, her daughter went on, "And these very private conversations. I don't understand."

"Have you asked the questions you need to ask?" her mother persisted, displaying attractively polished nails as she gesticulated. A well-ordered woman, she had chosen a shopping dress with an orange background and decorated with roses of various colours.

This 'well-deserving pensioner' was bent on enjoying herself.

"No."

"Why not?"

"I am honestly a little afraid of what I will learn."

"I know what you are saying," her mother responded as though from a distance. Her mouth stiffened with some deep, unreadable emotion, and she strained her mind for the right answers.

"But since you are obviously so troubled, you have to be brave and probe gently. Try not to lose your cool or act suspicious."

Her daughter was surprised at the deep passion with which she spoke. She desperately wanted to ask about the past that had produced such emotion. It was a revealing yet uncomfortable moment in which each felt trapped in a maelstrom from which she struggled to escape.

As they rose from the table she said to her mother, "Maybe I should try again for a child."

Her mother paused thoughtfully, before responding. She knew this was the prelude to another meeting which must be soon. "Be sure you know what you're doing," she said, really concerned.

They parted with the understanding that she was going to worry less and discreetly observe her husband. Their long, warm, emotional embrace was mutually comforting.

Today, having finished his meal, Dirk carried out the ritual well-known by those in his circle. He made a few quick trips taking the dishes back to the kitchen. Then he packed away the leftovers and washed the dirty dishes. This was something she liked about him. He was neat. Momentarily, they worked in companionable silence which was only disrupted by his unexplained comment about a woman who had dismembered her husband with a knife as sharp as hers. She stopped working, wondering why he would make such an odd remark. The picture he painted brought out an involuntary laugh which surfaced as a high-pitched hollow sound. He just looked at her curiously before leaving the kitchen.

This rejuvenating journey was just what she needed, what they both needed. Her troubled spirits were soothed by the natural beauty around them. It was so pervasive that even the average traveller could not avoid it. The hillsides to the left were covered with a beautiful haze of yellow-brown plant canopy etched artistically against the blue-white glazed skies. Here and there the sky was decorated with frothy white formations which were true of a day that was so perfect. In the country, you could not help being conscious of the overarching sky, the clouds, the trees and the feel of the air.

The other side of the road had a few houses straddling the low, undulating hills with the sea as backdrop, just lying there. It just lay there for most of the journey, silvery blue disturbed only now and then with a long, bubbling ripple that dissipated before reaching the shore. But she recalled other times when it was as silent as the grave. Further on, the sea decided to show its presence with little waves lapping rhythmically against the shore and suggesting an equilibrium she was longing for.

He cast a swift, oblique glance at her, his brow knitted in an inexplicable frown. It was such a fleeting look that she did not succeed in connecting with his eyes, something she desperately needed. They had driven over twenty silent miles and she felt an intense longing for conversation but did not have the courage to start one. The small puff of grey cloud ahead of them gave her the icebreaker she so urgently needed. Trying not to sound alarmed, she ventured, hesitantly touching the arm next to her on the wheel.

"Hope that," she said, pointing to the cloud, "does not mean rain."

"Mmm."

"The beach is kinda damp when it rains," she said, laughing at her own joke.

"I suppose it is," he said in a tone that suggested that he thought her comment was stupid.

"Just joking," she said.

"Yeah."

The brief window had closed, and he had deliberately turned his focus once more to the road.

The beach was as warm as one would have liked it to be. They laid out their belongings under a palm tree that provided shade from the burning heat of the sun. And the heat was otherwise tempered by the insistent, cool sea breeze intensified by the huge waves that dashed incessantly onto the shore. Even the towels they spread out felt warm to the skin from the pebbles underneath. She was soon in the water dawdling, and displaying for as long as seemed reasonable, her brief bikini on her very attractive form while he sat in morose silence on the shore. He had said from the first time they met that she had a figure that would not change and indeed, even after ten years of marriage and two miscarriages, she had maintained her form.

She soon admitted to herself that she was posing in vain and dove into the welcoming water. It enveloped her lovingly, caressing her skin and easing away the tension. As she took smooth, gentle strokes away from the shore, he receded from her consciousness. Now she lay on her back, eyes closed and welcomed the tender warmth of the sun on her face. This is heaven, she thought as she drifted. I love heaven! She alternated between closing and opening her eyes to make sure she did not drift too far away. She could swim but not powerfully, so she was careful.

Being in the water by herself was less fun than she wanted and after a while she headed for shore. She knew she made a picture he loved, her form dripping wet and seductive. Walking gingerly towards him on the sand, she shouted, "Dirk! Let's walk!"

For a while she got no answer although he looked at her. Really looked at her, she thought.

"It's beautiful down the beach." Hope sounded in her voice as she drew close to him.

"I'll pass," he said.

"Well..." she paused, her face clouded in disappointment as she turned, unable to continue, then walked away, back along the beach.

The walk allowed her to reach out to nature all around her. She stretched her imagination to what existed beyond the thick growth of trees before the beach front. She laughed at the sea gulls swooping down into the water. And she cried a little at her feeling of helplessness.

When she was spent, she returned to the picnic spot, sensing that he was more relaxed. He spread the picnic towel, spooned cubes of ice into large disposable cups and poured the lemonade she had made. Both consumed lunch from individual kits while the sun quickly and efficiently dried her bathing suit. She was encouraged but reluctant to venture into conversation other than the very casual.

"More chicken, Dirk?" she asked, pointing to the extra food in the carrier.

His reply was, "I'm fine."

"Ready for the water?"

"Not quite. You go," he said, barely glancing at her scantily clad body now.

"I'll wait a while," she said, watching hesitantly while he put everything away. Feeling a little drowsy, she formed her hands into a head rest, placed them behind her on the towel and leaned back. Soon she got into a mild doze. When she woke up, he was not there, and she looked curiously around. There were only two other couples and an ad hoc group a little farther down the beach. Well, she thought, he must have gone for a walk somewhere or to make one of his favourite calls. The water was once again welcome relief from the sun on her skin and the hurt in her heart.

It was much rougher now with the frequency of the waves seeming to have doubled since she was last in. She bobbed up and down with the waves, screaming in delight every time one washed over her. If only she had learnt to surf, it would have been great. She could only imagine that pleasure. Something rough brushed her thigh and she jumped uncontrollably thinking it was a shark, but it was only a piece of black driftwood, no doubt washed from shore, and soggy and peeling from the battering by the waves. She looked thoughtfully at it, wondering how long it would survive the ongoing onslaught. It seemed to have resided in the rough, watery habitat for a long time. Then a huge wave overcame her and when she surfaced the wood was an almost indistinguishable object dipping aimlessly up and down in the distance.

Dirk had surfaced and was now on the shore in his trunks. As always, he made her stomach tighten with his virile, lean, strong frame. He was an avid outdoor walker, taking to the hills with his friends every weekend, meaning Saturday and Sunday, when they travelled miles in the early morning. Apart from that they went to the gym religiously at least twice per week. He was coming into the water, and she allowed a little flicker of hope as she counted on the tranquil and inspiring atmosphere to stimulate the long-desired interaction with him.

She watched him walk, his long brawny legs cutting effortlessly through the shallow water until he started swimming lazily towards her as if he was taunting her. He knew she was waiting. He knew her so well. When he reached her, she gently held his hand and started to urge him further, she herself swimming easily by his side. She looked at him briefly and caught his eyes, distant, inscrutable. The semblance of a smile played about his mouth but did not reach his eyes. Her mind became confused, and she remembered him speaking on his cell phone one night and promising trips to the country. He was talking about someone being cloistered... needing to break out. He was going to do it. She squeezed her eyes shut for a moment, willing herself to shut out the memories and the questions.

A dark cloud had crept unnoticed across the sky, casting a large shadow over the area. The breeze had gradually become cooler, but the water was still warm. A huge wave washed over them and in surfacing, they pulled apart. He was still swimming away as though she was beside him, plunging further into the dark blue depths, leaving her behind. Before she could move, another wave covered her and when she surfaced, he was farther out. She felt panic overtaking her and she screamed out his name again and again with all the strength in her lungs, "Dir—K! Dir—K!" But in horror she saw him going under and then surfacing, so he could not hear her. Her voice became weaker after every submergence, and she felt it was no use. She did not think she would have the strength to swim back to the shore. The waves were now a riot, crashing thunderously towards the shore and making it difficult for her to balance enough to swim, but her mind kept saying, *you have to move.*

She did a back flip towards the shore. That got her nowhere, but she was too scared to turn her back to the deep sea. It seemed to be pulling her in. She tried another flip that seemed to have helped a little, but by the time she could marshal her thoughts a huge wave crashed over her, and she seemed to have advanced a little further towards the shore. But the backwash posed a problem and she prayed that the breakers would not become so powerful that her progress would be cancelled. The next wave was what she feared. It was a giant gush of blue and white that seemed to reach up to the skies as it surged forward, breaking much further than any of the others and sending huge streams of water onto the sand. She grew frantic at the thought of what could happen and with all the energy she could find, she dove into the water moving forward on the best backstroke she had ever executed.

"Where is the man that was with her?" someone asked. And then someone said, "O my Father, look out there!"

Fighting the waves was her husband. She started crying. She felt someone holding onto her upper body but she was too weak to react or care who it was. The person was pulling her forward as he skilfully treaded water. Like a drunken man without control of his motions, she listlessly lay in the arms of her rescuer. Her heartbeat quickened when she thought of her husband. Where was he? She started to cry and painfully expelled loads of water through her nose and mouth. She realised she could not have gone another yard on her own. The waves were really rough now, but she felt safe.

Her rescuer placed her on a deck chair and a woman that seemed to be his companion came over, followed by a little group that seemed to come from nowhere.

For the first time, she saw the man who had taken her in. He was surprisingly young and strong, and very concerned.

"He is a good swimmer. He will fight. Try to pray for him," he encouraged her.

"Would you like some tea?" The lady who was obviously his companion rushed to get a warm cup of mint from their thermos, but all her tumultuous thoughts were on the advancing figure in the furious waters. Someone placed her in a sitting position as he pitted his strength against the turbulent tide. A chorus of "Go Dirk! Go Dirk!", was carried across the rough wind and waves. Those were heart stopping moments for her and she could only muster a weak incoherent sound occasionally. The cruel waves kept lashing him as though they wanted to break his will, but they did not know him well. He was going to make it ashore.

After long, frightening minutes he seemed to gain ground and was definitely moving to shore. The little group started clapping and others further down the beach joined them and clapped, and soon it was a veritable welcoming party. "Dirk! Dirk! Dirk!" rang out insistently with each stroke of his tiring arms.

One man rushed towards the water, poising himself to jump in, and eagerly met him as he came stumbling in and collapsed exhausted on the sand next to her. She breathed easier but the tension in her stomach made it difficult for her to do anything except just hold his hand. For a few minutes, neither of them spoke. He was just sore from the effort.

Everyone was asking questions.

"What happened?"

"Why did you take so long out there?"

"Did you forget the woman?"

He ignored the questions and turning towards her asked, "Are you okay?"

She could only nod. Satisfied, he turned to the audience, speaking to no one in particular,

"You know," he said gasping with each word, "I have never experienced such strong waves at this beach. It's so strange. One minute I was holding her hand and the next minute I was battling to prevent myself from being swallowed up in a whirlpool."

The young man looked at him questioningly. "But the whirlpool is about thirty feet away. Did you go that far?"

"It is nearer than you think," he said, getting annoyed and wanting to just rest. For the first time, he looked at her.

The young man looked at him in disbelief. "I know this water like the back of my hand," he said simply and nudged his companion to leave them alone.

"You do not know the water at this time of day," his companion answered, surprised at his insinuation. "Let's be glad they are both alive."

"Hey," Justine interjected, breaking the tension, "I need to thank you properly. Please give me a contact number."

The rescuer's companion reached into her beach bag for a notebook from which she tore a piece of paper to write the information. The group drifted away, leaving good wishes for their future.

Alone now, and emotionally and physically drained, they sat on the sand looking out at the sea. Her mind was clouded by uncertainties as she looked vacantly at the forbidding waves relentless in their thrashing of the docile shore. The sun was slipping towards the horizon but it was still fairly warm. They looked curiously at each other — survivors both and each with a myriad of questions. Without a word they went to the picnic spot and gathered their beach bags and lunch kits. After placing the kits in the car, they went to the restrooms where they dressed for home.

The journey home seemed interminable. She had no reaction to the cool, evening breeze and the steady drizzle outside. Even a near collision sparked no reaction from her. Her mind was abuzz with questions.

With great determination she said, "Let's stop for a while. I need to talk to you."

'Now?" was his query. "Aren't you anxious to get home? I have no further explanation. Something must be brewing farther out for the water to have behaved so unusual."

"I have passed that matter. I guess the young man was just worn from anxiety. Forgive him. But this matter is still with us."

He slowed beside a fruit stand. "Do you want fruits?" he asked superficially. He was obviously relieved to have parked beside the fruit vendor but not surprised that she saw the fruits as a distraction.

"No, I just want to talk."

He waited.

"Well, I don't understand what's been going on. You don't want to talk. You are distant and curt. Then you have so many secret conversations. Then we come to the beach, and I thought we could reach an understanding, but the elements seemed determined to prevent that." She made an almost imperceptible shift of her position, looking at him through narrowed eyes. She saw his face harden before he started to respond.

"Were you thinking that ...?"

"Yes," she said.

She held her breath as he said, "I can't blame you. I've not shared this problem because I've been trying to sort it out."

Her brows furrowed. "What?"

"Before we met, I had a daughter who is in very delicate mental health. I am busy trying to place her somewhere, especially since her mother died."

Her bulging eyes showed her alarm. "I don't believe this. We promised not to keep secrets." She was uncharacteristically watchful. "I can't believe you have kept this from me. I am your wife, not just a ..." she said, her voice breaking.

Although she tried, she lost the battle to prevent the flood of tears that flowed unabated down her cheeks and onto his hand which was constantly mopping like a tireless windscreen wiper. He allowed the flow to subside and her heaving chest to gradually become less agitated. Then he folded her like a baby in his arms, resting his cheek on her shoulder.

Woman-like, she continued, "I would never imagine that you could not trust me..." her voice tapered off as her eyes smarted again.

"Sweetheart, I know I messed up badly but hear me out." His voice was a little muffled because his lower jaw rested on her shoulder. "I just did not want to burden you or disappoint you. It's hard to explain." He dug his chin into her shoulder as her pain became his. He could go on no more. She leaned her head against him, giving him the support she saw him needing. This was no time for acrimony, no time for unforgiveness.

"It would not have been a secret for much longer because after several agonising weeks, I am finding a solution. So I've been far away in thoughts but not with another woman. There is no need for that, and I would not do that."

She sensed a closing off on the issue, and she looked at him in sudden understanding. His face no longer seemed remote and cold. Although the rain had intensified outside, the heater warmed the interior of the car, resulting in a cosy relaxed atmosphere. She felt rather than saw him glance at her sideways from time to time and knew that she need not ask any more questions.

She reached over and squeezed his hand in reassurance. “Let’s go home,” she urged quietly.

The Report

Jerrie walked uncertainly towards the doctor's office situated on the second floor of the two-storey building. The doctor had said three weeks, but she just could not wait any longer. The brightly polished mahogany door opened in response to her buzz, and she hesitated before going in. After all, it was not yet time, she reasoned, suddenly confused about her rather brash decision.

Several seconds passed and then with an unexpected gush of determination, Jerrie stepped resolutely into the familiar waiting area, where, thankfully, the only other patient was a middle-aged, slightly greying lady who sat crossed-legged on the colourful office couch, engrossed in a magazine.

She liked that the receptionist did not even glance at her. The woman sat authoritatively in the midst of an array of files, arranged in cubicles on the wall behind her, and patient cards filed neatly in the cabinet against the wall to her right. There were boxes of stuff on the floor before it, a pile of obviously unsorted mail on her large, L-shaped desk, and an unobtrusive glass-door cabinet to her right. Pausing from ruling a page in a large, three-quire notebook, she looked up, gave Jerrie her detached but friendly professional smile, and enquired how she might help.

"I am Jerrie Myers and I have an appointment for the day after tomorrow. I know you said I should call tomorrow or even the following day for the results," she said, almost in a whisper. "But since I was in the area, I thought I might as well pop by." Her tone was apologetic, and her words low and uncertain as she barely managed to control their urgency and her rising hysteria.

She hoped the valiant attempt at sounding casual had worked. She hoped the beads of sweat on her forehead did not show but she did not want to reveal her discomfort by wiping her face. Her stomach felt like it housed a hundred riotous blackbirds which could be heard by anyone several feet away.

The receptionist asked Jerrie to sign the register on the counter and reached for the pile of mail on the desk. "Bingo," she said, smiling as she raised a letter-sized brown envelope. "I will see if Doctor can be with you soon, Mrs Myers," she offered, giving her warm recycled smile before disappearing smoothly into an inner office, and returning in a few minutes just as smoothly to her desk in the cubicle which clearly defined her role. While Jerrie waited, the receptionist extracted her file and took it inside, and giving what was meant to be a reassuring smile, indicated that she should sit down.

The receptionist resumed her routine of reviewing each of the cards in the stack on the desk, and cross checking them with information on several sheets of paper lying on the table. Then every so often, she rose to place a little box of cards in her cabinet. For a while, the room was animated only by the ticking of the clock on the wall, and the crisp rustling of the paper disturbed by continuous breeze from the lazily whirring fan that sat prominently on the cabinet.

Jerrie wondered why the doctor was taking so long with the patient who had gone in before. As each expectant minute dragged by, she was overcome by a fervent need to occupy her mind. The familiar pictures on the wall became objects of careful new study. She wondered at the cause of the emotional turmoil being experienced by the character in the abstract painting entitled 'Woman'. *Lost love, broken dreams, anxiety over decisions – poor woman, poor all of us women*, she lamented silently, feeling almost overwhelmed by a fierce rush of empathy.

As she strove to further occupy her troubled mind, Jerrie's focus shifted to the drawings of the physiological systems. Not being science-oriented, she had always found each picture a learning experience, especially the familiar male form with its proud display of maleness, which at other times had held her attention more than any other. But on this day, her mind was unable to sustain the usual interest, and she felt her impatience growing as untamed as Jack's beanstalk. Her tumultuous thoughts thrashed around in her brain with negative, unbounded energy, and she took to mindlessly rocking back and forth to the rhythm of the clock... waiting and rocking, waiting and rocking. Just as she became exhausted from trying to relax, the clear, crisp voice of the doctor penetrated her fuzzy mind. The receptionist instantly raised her head and looked encouragingly at her. "Mrs Myers, you may go in now," she said.

Doctor Ross, a slightly greying woman of about sixty, sat coolly at her desk leafing through a file Jerrie assumed was hers. The doctor smiled without looking up and invited her to sit in the guest chair. Again, Jerrie tried to appear calm and casual.

"I was really in the area," she said, nervously brushing a stray strand of damp hair from her forehead, "and wondered if you had got my test results..." Her voice trailed off into a whisper.

"That's fine. Your particulars just arrived so I'll take a look shortly. But are you okay? Have you been keeping well? How is work?" Not waiting for an answer, she pre-empted her, "You look well."

"Yes," she said, forcing a weak smile that reached no further than her lips. She did not know what she was answering to. The doctor looked at Jerrie from a face that was as untouched as a freshly painted wall.

"Any specific problem since we spoke?" The doctor was looking carefully at the document on her desk. To Jerrie, the doctor was making great effort at small talk. It was clear that she was more interested in the file before her than in the emotional state of the patient sitting in front of her.

"None, really. I'm fine."

"Good. Two minutes are all I need," she offered before lapsing into another quick review of the document in her hand. It seemed like several minutes went by while she read the document with slightly knitted brows, underlining sections with a pencil which she held poised between her fingers. She then abruptly rose from her seat, and with her expression as bland as before, and a quick "soon come", went through the door into the outer room.

Jerrie managed a taut little smile because a response was expected. Her chest was an overfilled balloon that would burst at the slightest touch. The release she needed seemed to come from her foot-tapping exercise that soon gave way to a two-finger musical on the very edge of the table.

Jerrie's insides felt like a wound-up clock and the room became a blur of objects that had previously engaged her attention on the wall – certificates, all so impressive with their calligraphic beauty and the qualifications they certified – University of the West Indies, University of New Orleans, University of ...

Glancing towards the door, she thought the doctor was taking an awful long time to emerge with the paper. Had there been a mistake? Was it really there?

The room was extremely quiet. Her eyes flitted from the notebooks, files and pen, which were the only contents of the small prim table, to the filing cabinet in the corner on which stood two sparklingly clear glasses, each covered with a coaster along with a thermos. Soon her restless mind became a growing whirlpool of troubled thoughts and she became unsure about her ability to deal with any negative news. Something seemed to be urging her to go but she could not summon the energy to rise. Then the door opened and she looked involuntarily at the doctor's hand, unable to feign indifference.

The doctor slipped neatly into her place behind the desk.

"Sorry for the wait but I thought I would have finished with that file in less time," she said, looking reassuringly at Jerrie. "But now I'm all yours." She picked up another file from her desk, opened and perused it quickly, thoughtfully. Not once did she glance at Jerrie who was waiting almost open-mouthed. Then she opened the envelope. No emotion. Why did her action seem so staged? Or was it her imagination? Jerrie tried in vain to slow her quickening heartbeat.

She looked again at the envelope in the doctor's hand, trying to be calm. *Expect the worst*, a little voice said. *Be hopeful, another said. Whatever happens, the moment is now.* Cold reasoning took over. The doctor is taking a long time to open the envelope, but is there any hurry? Jerrie asked herself in confusion.

"It seems this came a short while ago," she said, deftly easing the flap of the envelope free with her letter opener. "Your timing is perfect," she continued with a hint of a smile.

With a smooth motion, she extracted the folded paper, spread it open and quickly looked at it and then back at the open file. For a few seconds, Jerrie did not breathe. The doctor was scanning the paper thoughtfully, her eyes never once leaving the page. Her professional demeanour firmly in place, she raised her head to meet the eyes of the woman across from her.

When the doctor raised her head, she was curiously contemplative as she looked Jerrie in the face. She paused like a golfer calculating how to get the ball into the waiting hole.

"The news is not what either of us would like. The test is positive." She hesitated, carefully choosing her words but not wanting to be seen to be doing so. "But don't for one moment, think it is the end of the world," she said quickly, too quickly, Jerrie thought, looking from the paper to her and seemingly trying not to sound too serious or too sad or too casual. It took Jerrie only a few seconds to realise that what she dreaded was confirmed. It took her less time to emit a painful "Oh God!"

"I know it's not the best news ever..." The doctor noticed Jerrie staring blindly at something behind her. She tried again. "Many people are surviving with this health problem. Care..." She stopped abruptly, concerned about Jerrie's reaction. She had seen that look before. It was the look of someone beaten.

Poor doctor, Jerrie thought, deliberately refocusing. She was not going to fall apart — not just yet. In fact, she was not surprised, just coldly resigned to what had just been a confirmation. A strangled chuckle escaped her. It was an early sign of the onset of hysterics, but she desperately wanted to be calm. Her fixed stare at the doctor was intent on keeping her hazy thoughts comprehensible.

She vaguely saw the neatly combed processed hair pulled into a French roll, expensive professional-looking glasses — black square frames and crystal-clear lenses worn on a noncommittal face. Jerrie felt helpless as an uncontrolled gurgle escaped from her, ending in a cranked-up smile.

She thought the doctor looked well-kept for her age, but poor soul, she could not stop the fine lines under her neck nor her eyes. I'm sure, she thought spitefully, if she could prevent the sagging of those arms, she would. The thoughts surfaced from somewhere in her mind but found no resonance with her true feelings about the doctor. She became instantly repentant, admitting to herself in shame that the doctor had just done her job. The doctor's voice firm and insistent, intruded, "Would you like me to give you a sedative and let you come back tomorrow?"

Jerrie could find no answer.

"May I call someone at home for you? You really should not be driving..."

Rebellion like a flood again welled up inside her. You can say anything, she thought. You are okay. She wanted to ask, "Doctor, have you ever taken an HIV test?" and watch her reaction carefully, but perhaps that sort of question does not come from a patient to her doctor, she thought in uncertainty. Oh yes, she is so perfect sitting down in her comfortable chair, undisturbed by the realities people like me face. I wish she knew what it's like, she thought, less out of spite and more out of the effort to ease her torment and keep sane. The blur in her mind grew larger and larger, and she found it increasingly difficult to complete her line of thought.

The doctor's voice, calm and clinical, penetrated only the outer layers of her mind. She was saying a lot of things about drugs, exercise, diet and support groups. She went on about health checks, about not being at death's door... Jerrie was thankful for the blankness of her mind. It was useful for now. Let tomorrow take care of itself, she insisted to herself.

There was a look of surprise on the doctor's face when she abruptly rose from her seat. "I have to go."

"No, you shouldn't just yet."

"I have to go," she repeated, moving resolutely towards the door.

"I'll take you," the doctor said. "Someone will take your car home."

She spoke to Jerrie hoping, it seemed, to delay her for a while longer.

"You need instructions, information, networking contacts. You need your first prescription and appointment. Please."

Jerrie felt she would explode if she lingered for another moment. A series of snickers escaped as she imagined her brains and entrails running down the doctor's face and white overcoat.

Blindly, she headed to the door and out into the busy street. The blustery wind just managed to temper the blistering heat of the early afternoon sun. But she plunged in, determined to submerge herself in any discomfort — pain drowning pain. This was a different reality to replace her reality. She looked back briefly to see the doctor framed in the doorway, a look of defeat on her usually composed face.

A Wish Only

It was the familiarity of the gait that got my attention. I had not seen this man in forty years, but I would recognise that unique walk anywhere. With arms swinging in time with the quick, smooth steps of his long bandy legs, he strode purposely from the entrance of the bus terminus. At times, he glided towards a cluster of persons waiting at a particular stop and peered intently into that group. I watched his actions, thinking at one point that this was just an idle exercise, and he was just curious and not really looking at anything. Just as in those days, I was fascinated by the intensity of his observation. In conversation, his gaze would be fixed on your face as though this were the most important activity he had ever undertaken. The same scrutiny was brought to bear on the waiting crowds. From his protruded face and restless roaming eyes, an onlooker would reasonably conclude that he was looking for something.

I watched unnoticed, certain that his eyes would meet my curious ones at any moment. I held my breath. But he passed me and after proceeding a few feet along the pavement, he stopped and then seemed to disappear somewhere in the cluster at the end of the pavement. However, a short while later he popped out from some place lower down and then he was coming again. I thought as I reviewed the long, dark, wandering face, time has done you well.

He was greying now, some wrinkles were evident too. He was also slimmer but had maintained a straight posture. He still wore clothes that were very becoming, casual but attractive. I wondered why he was roving about the bus park as though he had lost something that had to be found. He seemed oblivious to the deep, throbbing noise of the park and to the discordant actions of the bystanders in progress. He kept a pensive mobile stance. But as riveting as the scene was, I seemed to be the only one paying any attention to the quiet drama. I was caught between the world I knew yesterday and the scene unfolding before me now.

It seemed like just yesterday, he, along with Bunny and Maisie and me, were sitting in jolly relaxation at the large table stacked with white rum, vodka, sodas, and all manner of snacks so placed that they could be reached at any time. This was a fun place our group visited on some weekends or holidays. It was perfect, situated by the sea, its tranquillity undisturbed by other pleasure seekers. It was only one of our several haunts and carried an unmatched atmosphere of cosy homeliness. We were not a portrayal of sophistication. We were just a very earthy, sportive crew of working young adults who were bored by Friday evening every week, and wanted to unwind for the next forty-eight hours.

"Selene, the matchmaker," quipped Carly to the uproarious support of the others.

I kept a straight face but knew there was no escape. I felt the warmth of Sonny's breath on my neck as he peered into my uncertain hand. I was sure they all knew it was more than just a domino moment.

"No, Sonny. No cheating. You can't play for both of you," warned loud-mouthed Billy.

"Listen, you all. I am the best matcher around!" I had finally found my voice, but they knew my style and I was out of the game soon, as they had expected.

The poignancy of the interactions was so absorbing that I felt the moment would never end — the country-style food, the juices and the occasional dip in the ocean — an idyll not experienced in many places. It bore no sign of opulence but was just rustic and wholesome, and satisfactory to a group of lower-level professionals seeking clean adventure and a way of establishing an eternal bond. The closeness of the relationships in the group absorbed us, making the three couples which it comprised indistinct to all with whom we had cursory contact.

One Sunday, after much hilarity at one of our favourite beaches, we got out of the water, tired and famished. With understandable haste, we washed under the pipes provided and made our way to the beach chairs where the bags with our belongings had been placed, only to discover that there were only two towels between us. All except Carly looked helpless.

"Okay, so let the guys dry first and then we girls go," she said so casually you would think we did this all the time.

Altogether, we related as closely as siblings in a family but within the general friendship, we did not downplay the relations between each couple and the tacit understanding regarding boundaries between couples. So, the looks of raw affection between Sonny and me or the times he playfully pulled my hair or playfully nipped my shoulder was only met with a knowing smile from the others.

It was not until much later that I realised why we had been so interesting to the others. I was the youngest, fresh out of high school and was just being inducted into the world of work and adulthood. The others were more mature and longer established couples whose relationships were warm and settled. They were beyond footsy under the table or holding hands to walk along the rough path to the river at another of our favourite places.

One day as we travelled back from the beach, I sat with Sonny in the back while the others paired up in the front and middle seats.

"Hey, you lovebirds round there! What's up? We not hearing anything!" Billy, who was driving, shouted in competition with the rushing wind.

"Man, keep your eyes on the highway. See how long and tricky it is. You have no time to fast in people business."

"That's what you say," answered Billy. "I know this road like the path between my gate and my house."

At that, Carly, his companion, turned to everyone. "He's right. One extra drink and he doesn't know the path he's talking about."

"Lord, Carly, you cyaan stand up for me," he said, looking at her in mock annoyance.

The rest of us enjoyed the exchange, and Bunny and Maisie, started to sing, "Billy, keep your mind on your driving, keep your eyes on the road..."

My relationship with Sonny had been very fulfilling, especially after he had settled matters with my rival who thought the strength of her relationship with him lay in the strength of her female gang which she brandished when we crossed paths in the nearby town. Indeed, there was tension mixed with pleasure when my group of co-workers and I passed the raffish set of gangsters on the road.

"They are so loud," Annette, the obvious leader of my clique, said one day as they passed us laughing raucously and behaving very showy with their overdone gestures among them, and the brazen display of sexuality in their dress and manner of walking.

"You didn't tell him he has to get rid of the wench?" asked another friend, and my strongest ally, who obviously scorned the behaviour she was witnessing.

"I will not be in any argument with anyone. He has to choose now," I declared with a resolute air my friends loved.

And he did. He turned out to be a caring, sweet personality: a man like other men, but at the same time, respectful of my wishes.

I had grown up in a quiet, slow-moving village where most children graduated from all-age school with few options. Fortunately, a few of us from our cohort qualified for places in the most prominent high school in the parish. After school, I had decided or rather was pushed into teaching much against my wishes, but I had little desire to appear ungrateful to my teacher and benefactor who was head of the school I had attended where I took my first job. Poor but ambitious, I had decided early that babies would not be on my agenda for a long time. The examples of educated family members who had started in dwellings as lowly as thatched houses, inspired me with the notion that life had more experience to offer than a baby by my side. In fact, I was so driven by this resolution that I refused to satisfy the requests of the young men around who confused my friendly responses with some unspoken understanding of my intention to satisfy their curiosity.

Sonny was the perfect gentleman who would not move one step further than I would go. We did the movies, parties, lunches and the beach without a shred of discomfort. And we continued along those lines when we both migrated to the big city. We had left the other two couples in the country, and we were both occupied, me in college and he in work as a detective. But where the wind would blow, no one knew. Nor could we tell from whence it came. At least, I could not at the time; but in retrospect, there were seeds of uncertainty sown by both of us.

"Why you looking at me so?" Sonny was asking as he spooned rice from the dish onto my plate.

"No reason," I said, not wanting to admit my sudden flash of fear nor to show that my eyes were a little misty.

"You are a strange girl." He chuckled as he started to eat, with me following suit, but glancing for some unexplained reason at him every so often. His face was not by any stretch of the imagination handsome, but it was interesting with a big mouth, thick lips and a straight long nose. The overall reddish-brown look of the eyes, eyebrows and moustache, completed that unique and yet appealing appearance that I had found hard to resist.

"Sweets, you will have to tell me."

"Not now," I said, feeling rather foolish.

"I'm seeing you later, right? So no getting away." He had come back with the familiar endearing look.

But I did not have any concrete reason to be disturbed until the rumour surfaced.

After class one day, I was walking in companionable silence with a fellow student on the college compound when she volunteered.

"My dear, you heard the story?"

"No. What?" I asked, not very excited.

"I hear that this girl, Charm, who is in the mathematics department met a guy at a party and they had an instant affair. Remember the Santa Anna High School old students party two weeks ago? "

"Yes, I do. I did not go because I was doing an assignment that couldn't wait," I replied, thinking I had missed the excitement.

Sonny had not been pleased because it was an occasion to which I was the one who invited him at first.

"She had better hope our head of department is kept in the dark."

"You know what that would be," I said, knowing exactly what.

"I think the guy is a detective. I hear he is attractive and ..."

I could not comment, but waited, hardly breathing for the rest of the story. I knew. He had only called me once in two weeks and I had thought he was just busy with a new job. Like any other woman, I did not want to acknowledge such a thing. I wished she had not told me. Luckily for me, most persons in my circle had no knowledge of my relationship. It was gut-wrenching for me. It was as if my future had somehow become unattractive. Where was the tall dark man in it?

There followed a dark period of pain, disillusionment and separation. The usual calls did not come. Nor did the dates. However, one evening, a few months after I had completed my course and was at my new home, a vehicle pulled up at my gate. To my surprise and distress, it was Sonny. That visit ended prematurely. I could not go back.

As I looked at Sonny now, I tossed around in my mind the idea of calling to him, remembering that I had seen him twice before and on one of those occasions, he said he did not remember who I was. I actually felt very sorry for him then, thinking that it was the ageing thing. Now I had to make up my mind. And I decided to just live in the now. The happenings recalled were in the distant past and I had put those behind a long, long time ago.

"Hello, Mr Williams," I said, stepping into his now well-defined path.

He stopped and his glazed brown eyes swept over my face. "Selene," he said, using his finger to trace an imaginary frame for my face.

"Yes," I said. "You know who you are talking to?" I asked, knowing that my face had a puzzled look.

"Yes, Selene. Let's talk," he said, motioning for me to step aside.

I felt out of my depth. "Well," I explained with determined clarity, "I was just saying hi. Haven't seen you in quite a while."

"Selene, I wondered where you had gone to." He drew closer and I resisted the desire to look up.

"Oh, I have been here and there and living."

"Yes, you look so nice, no ageing, as cute as ever."

No blush. No words from either of us. We just looked at each other with undisguised curiosity.

Before he could say anything else, my bus came, and relieved, I quickly boarded. When I saw him follow me, I thought he was taking the same bus, but he was not. I leaned towards the door to hear him say, "No number?"

"No, no number," I said in genuine surprise.

"Yet," he said as the door closed.

"Never," I said to him as well as to myself, with a resolute ring to my deliberately low-pitched voice as the bus moved. "Ne-ver."

The Right Hand

Pauline did not know what she was expecting when she decided to participate in the church exchange programme. This was one of the few times her parents would have willingly allowed her to spend time away from her family, so it filled her with a sense of great excitement.

"Remember to be careful in the sea," her mother called, as she stepped into the city-bound bus.

"Yes Mama," she responded, fearing that the whole bus had heard the unnecessary reminder.

It was the first time she would be away from home for all of three days and it would be her first time at a tourist resort. She considered herself very lucky to have been included in such a thrilling affair, pregnant with possibilities that she could not specify at the moment. In a state of confused excitement, she pushed clothing, too much, into her bag which all of a sudden, looked very ordinary.

"I'm sorry that this is the only bag I can get," she complained to her mother who had come into her room.

"Don't worry. It's not bad," her mother consoled her. "Just be the girl I brought up. Your behaviour matters more."

She was not sure of the clothes either. *Are they okay?* she wondered. Although brought up in what was considered a very liberal church, even a non-Christian church by some, she was conservative, some might even have said, prissy. She kept her fun within boundaries defined mainly by her parents who kept the high ambitions they had for her dangling before her all the time.

At fifteen, she was on the cusp of womanhood. One more year in high school and then she would be out into the open world. For this, her expectations were developed mainly from the several stern lectures from her parents and teachers, all of whom displayed little skill in imparting the lessons needed by an unexposed, poor but promising young girl. However, her well-meaning parents did not recognize that much of her understanding of life was supplied by her dinky collection of romance and mystery novels, coupled with magazines' light, shallow stories and her uncle's not-so-subtle notebooks, left in his library. She perused all voraciously. But while she was curious, some experiences common to some of her peers remained uncharted paths for her.

Going to spend a night in a prime residential area, and then meeting a co-participant from Florida, was a novel experience. The area was unlike anywhere she had been, so different from her country district. In her area, there were only a few scattered opulent homes that stood like lonely lighthouses in the generally depressed neighbourhoods. Here, the houses were all neatly painted, mainly in pastel colours with well-kept lawns and gardens adorned with breath-taking flowers, many of which she had never seen before.

She became so lost in the beauty and affluence of the place that she could not remember the directions. *Silly me,* she thought, *how do I get to this house when there is no one in the yards for me to ask?*

Even though she glimpsed someone now and then, it was not easy to reach them given the long driveways leading to the houses which made her feel too distanced to connect with them in order to ask for information.

Just as she was getting scared that the afternoon would turn to evening, worsening her chances of finding the house, a police car drove up and stopped. She felt a weight lift from her weary shoulders now hurting from the heavy bag she had been moving from one to the other. Although there was normally no occasion in which she interacted with police cars in the country, she welcomed the chance to ask someone who must surely have the answer.

"Can we help you?" an officer asked, sticking his head through the window while the other looked on interestedly.

"I am trying to find 34 Rose Avenue where I will be spending the night en route to a church retreat," she said eagerly. She wanted to make sure that she did not give a bad impression or raise any doubts. There was no need for her to say another word.

"Okay, I know where. That's the home of Judge Morgan," said the officer, smiling. "Come along. We'll take you." It was as if he did that every day.

Pauline relaxed easily in the car, but felt very inadequate about the prospect of staying in the home of a judge. She did not know what to expect. After only about three minutes, she was gratefully disembarking from the car but unsure of her next steps.

If the judge or his wife recognized her unease, she did not know. There she was in the most splendid home she had ever been, being hosted by people she never thought she would ever meet, a judge, his urbane wife and a Caucasian girl from a world she did not know. This was a lot for her to absorb. She wondered several times during the evening whether she would fit in. Whereas the American girl was quite suave and sociable, she was definitely out of her depth. As girls tend to know one another, she thought that, at least the American would have sensed her humble background. She squirmed quietly, thinking she must be seeing through her plain pink 'little girl' dress that lacked any real style when compared with her trendy floral waist-length shirt and pedal pushers. She *must* be noticing my hesitant and cautious interventions in what for the others is fluent conversation, she thought.

"Miss Alva, it is a pleasure having you in Jamaica. First time?"

"Yes, sir. It is, and I can't wait to get to the coast. But please call me Yasmine."

"That's such a pretty name and you are a pretty girl. If you are not yet spoken for, I'm sure you will attract one of these church boys," the judge commented appreciatively. "I understand that over the years of this camp, some good matches have emerged."

For the first time Yasmine hesitated, seeming not to have been expecting such a personal comment. Pauline smiled politely as she tried unsuccessfully to find an entry point.

"Oh, sir, I have no interest. I just want to have fun."

The judge looked knowingly at his wife.

"Dear, can you tell her?"

"Don't listen to him," Mrs Morgan said. "He thinks he can see everybody's future. Girls, just have some great fun and take care of yourselves. No risks. It's a holiday but be mindful that you are a church group and we do not want a bad report."

"Trust my wife," the judge said in mock exasperation.

The judge was unreservedly mirthful as he casually spooned kale salad onto a small slice of homemade lasagne from what Pauline thought was a meagre dish since the only other ingredients were roasted cucumber slices. Everyone else seemed quite satisfied and unwillingly partook of the small soufflé that topped off the supper. After the meal, Pauline was still hungry, however. All her reserves of energy had dissipated while she was travelling for four hours from the country, along one of the most winding roads in the island. Now, she thought longingly of how much she would have welcomed her favourite home-made biscuits, with a warm cup of Milo.

Pauline thought that Mrs Morgan was sensitive to her hesitancy. She started a conversation with her, asking about her school, her parents and her country church. Like a drowning man she held onto that one-to-one exchange and in her own way, she encouraged it. Mr Morgan was enjoying his conversation without them, laughing from his belly bottom at the jokes Yasmine was giving. Pauline found it funny to see his belly shaking like a blob of jelly violently thrown into a dish. With each peal of laughter, the huge bulge rose to what seemed like a confirmed level, remained for a second or two, and then as the laughter died, it shook violently and came to a settled position once more.

She hesitated to join them for 'a glass of wine' on the patio. She did not want to be involved in a cosy chat with them sitting together on the long wrought-iron seat and the wine glasses lined up before them on the wrought-iron coffee table. But she did not know what to do next. She did not want to be impolite.

"Judge Clarke," she said, her voice a little shaky, " I am sorry but I am feeling tired and..." she paused.

"O yes, little one, you may go. Won't hold you. In the country you would be asleep now, eh?" the judge asked. Pauline thought he did not mind her going. So, she escaped before his wife returned.

When she had arrived earlier, Pauline had been introduced to the room, one of the twin bedrooms originally occupied by one of the two daughters raised in the house. It was a girl's dream with its frilly lace curtains, large dressing table with heart-shaped pink doilies matching the walls, a too-large close, and a double-bed dressed with a beautiful comforter and four fluffy pillows. She thought this was too lavish to be slept in. For the first time in her life, she had a bathroom all for herself. It did not matter that it would be for one night only. She loved the bathroom and would have happily slept on the soft, white rug but instead she heeded her rational mind — should Mrs Morgan check on her, what would she say?

All through the evening Pauline had sensed Mrs Morgan observing her. Was it in an understanding sort of way? She was not sure, but she did not want it to make her nervous. And so, she proceeded in preparing for her night's rest, taking time to do things and moving as quietly as she could, so as not to disturb the calmness of the surroundings. It was a dreamlike situation. The lights were on as though it was daylight and there was no sound except the occasional closing of a door or the soft-footed padding of feet on the wooden floors. But as she lifted the soap dispenser, the ill-fated bathroom fitting slipped from her careful fingers and fell with a loud thud on the carpet.

When Mrs Morgan appeared as if on cue, Pauline's hands were still in the air as though they were frozen there.

Her good feelings about Mrs Morgan were not unfounded.

"Oh, what happened? Are you okay?" she asked, moving closer to inspect Pauline's hands which as though by their own accord, had fallen to her sides.

"I... I..." Pauline stammered. "I have... had ... an accident," she said, looking from the broken soap dispenser to her hostess.

Pauline became very guarded when Mrs Morgan bent down to pick up the two pieces of porcelain. She waited in trepidation as the older woman rose with a look of concern on her usually pleasant features. Her brows were knitted, and she screwed her pink mouth to force out the words.

"This was a gift from me to Ailee. What did you do to it?" She looked Pauline straight in the face, with a look of disbelief and, without waiting for an answer, wheeled out of the room. Pauline tried to follow but only saw her loose-fitting floral blouse floating around a corner in the house where she was not sure she could go. So, rather than do something unacceptable to the bed, that night she slept on the rug. She wanted to make sure that in the morning the bed would be as immaculate as she had found it.

Departure in the morning could not come too soon. Pauline felt like a clumsy oaf. Not surprisingly, Mrs Morgan just wished her guests a good morning and bade them to have breakfast which was continental and swift – slices of brown bread, eggs delicately fried, oranges peeled and cut, and a steaming teapot.

"Mr Morgan is a late sleeper," the hostess said, looking more at Yasmine than at Pauline, which the latter was comfortable with.

"Oh, you will say farewell and thanks for us?" Yasmine asked, now including Pauline with her hazel eyes which the debutante looked at whenever she got an opportunity.

"I will. Hope you girls slept well." She paused by the table set by the unseen hand that had prepared the supper previously.

Yasmine was bright and expectant and chatty as she quickly drank a cup of tea and ate one side of the sandwich. She obviously wanted to be on the road.

Mrs Morgan appeared again and quickly surveyed the table.

"In this house," she said, "we do not throw away food, so I'll pack your fruits and what's left of your other stuff, and you can have this on the road." That was close to being an order.

"Now you can do the last bathroom rites and wait for your bus," she said, quickly disappearing again.

Pauline did not want another mishap. So, she quickly rinsed her mouth, straightened anything that seemed out of place and found herself in the dining area once more, just as Yasmine came excitedly out with her backpack.

There were two packages on the dining table, wrapped and waiting with the names on. And Mrs Morgan, the bustling hostess, was right at the door to greet the driver of the bus and say goodbye to everyone. This was the last of the moments Pauline dreaded. Yasmine, however, was one for hugs, and she set the pace.

"Mrs Morgan, you have been a great mother," Yasmine said, smiling at her hostess. She was so self-confident and so vivacious that Pauline felt a sense of foreboding.

"Mrs Morgan," she said, trying neither to be too light nor to be so contrite that it would stir up the bad feelings of the night before. "Thank you for accommodating us. It was interesting for me and ... I am really sorry about the mishap," she offered, looking her in the face and then quickly hugging her.

"My dear, these things do happen even to the best of us," Mrs Morgan said, returning the embrace. She shooed them out with a smile and it was clear she was trying to be practical and kind at the same time.

They waved to her from the bus filled with young persons from different places locally and abroad. People were greeting one another in excitement and Pauline could see some sparks flying in some places, but none for her. She felt happy to be away from home for a week but she was now very uncertain that she would fit in, and anticipated travelling a bumpy path when she would have to give an account of herself at the resort.

Part II

Pauline went to the resort with great reservation. Her feelings were as cold as the pine cabins in which the group would spend the next few days. While she felt happy that they had individual rooms thanks to their corporate church body, she felt cut off from the others who seemed to have struck up relationships by the time they got off the bus. Already, she could hear light-hearted chatter outside the cabin, and laughter erupting from the open areas. She hesitated before entering the outdoor dining area — who could she sit with? But really, it was not as painful as it seemed as she soon saw a familiar-looking table that seated four young ladies whom she learned were from churches in her part of the country. So, she relaxed.

"See you in thirty minutes... see you at supper...see you in a while... hurry down ya'll." The camaraderie after three hours of travel was already amazing and to no one's surprise, ballooned. An interesting seating arrangement emerged. A few 'couples' were immediately obvious such as Yasmine with a handsome local young man, who seemed to be very affected by the slim, caucasian girl with braided hair.

All through the evening, Pauline felt like an oddity. She just could not relax. She was again feeling unhappy with the clothes she had brought. Everyone looked so jazzy. She always seemed to be on the fringes of a group, not knowing where to turn for interaction. That was made particularly difficult because it was so informal. People switched seats to talk to those who interested them but she was glued to where she was. Boring, she thought. That's what I am. She wanted to creep away as soon as she could, to see if she could find an answer to her unique problem. And so, she did, not thinking that anyone would notice. And no one seemed to do so.

Pauline breathed deeply when she was inside the room at last. The calming colours of the walls and the curtains made it easy to release the tension that had dogged her all evening. The cold of the room was welcome. The television was good company, and she marvelled at being able to watch four hours of news, movies and soap operas, whatever she wanted. This was so unlike going to her friend's house and sharing a show with six or seven other persons on the veranda. She wrapped herself in the luxurious comforter and fumbled with the remote until she located a channel that she liked.

The dashing, roaring waves outside were non-threatening. They created a sense of being in an abysm in which the cabin was sitting. Pauline needed no contact now. She could drown herself uninterrupted in the offerings. She did not want to sleep. This needed to last for a long time.

Morning woke her up, cold and uncertain. She wanted food and she was quick to head for the dining room, now sparse with the group members and with other guests. When she had finished the meal, others were just coming in. She was glad to be leaving without having to try so hard to make conversation.

She did not need to be sociable in the session that followed. She actually enjoyed the talk and the question and answer although she hardly spoke. She could identify with the Christian teenage problems. How did they live in the world and not be a part of it? She was not convinced they were succeeding as she had seen so many behaviours that contradicted what the facilitator was saying.

The mingling was another opportunity for them to share freely before settling down for brief presentations. From then on, Pauline had someone to talk to, but she could not stay glued to anyone as her friends were able to move in outer circles. Every time she tried to break out, it seemed to end unfulfilled. Then they finished their morning devotion, introductory session and singalong which made her feel inconspicuous but a little warmer towards everyone because it was a group affair and required very little of her.

Lunch was rather nice. It was served on the patio, just a few feet above the sea lazily lapping a sweet-sounding welcome in its ebb and flow. Pauline basked in the warm, afternoon sun. Daring birds descended, at times perilously close to the diners, but the waiters, anxious to please, quickly shooed them off. The restful ambience made all anxiety seem evanescent, and she enjoyed stimulating conversation in which she and her companions shared stories about situations and persons that they all knew. It was oddly comforting.

This was a fun weekend so after lunch it was the pool decorated with a mélange of surprisingly skimpy bikinis, as well as some modest two and one pieces. Yasmine was having great fun with her special number, a short, slim, blonde American who was teaching some daring diving moves, and there was more pairing up than she could imagine. But Pauline found herself engaging in repartee with others she had not spoken to before, as she fooled around in the shallow end of the pool.

"Come on scaredy-cat. Get out of the children's section," a laughing young man from America teased, tugging at her arm. His wet brown hair lay limply at the nape of his neck and he was pressing his nose to release the water that had crept up there as he pulled her forward.

"Oh no, I can't. I don't know how to swim," she protested. She was conscious that the attention of some of the frolickers were on the two of them, and she did not know what to do. Say no, and she might miss the opportunity to be more integrated. Say yes and she might not manage.

"Come on," he urged. "I am a great teacher. Ask Dianne." At the mention of the name, he shouted, "Dianne! Come and give your testimony."

A Caucasian girl with short, cropped, black hair came swimming effortlessly towards them. She looked at Pauline encouragingly.

"You will not regret it. He makes a good teacher and a good brother."

"Well..."

"No, you won't drown," she said, getting ready to go back to her splashing, riotous circle.

"Okay," Pauline said, feeling that this was a moment being watched by everybody, even if they pretended otherwise. But by the time she got to a deeper section, she realized that not even the old student was paying her the least attention.

"I don't even know your name," she said, trying not to be reserved.

"Nor do I know yours, but we are allowed to be nameless."

"But you will be teaching me."

"So?"

"So, let's exchange names."

He was tickled into helpless mirth.

"So, let's be formal. Are you a teacher, by the way?"

"In training."

She was beginning to feel that she had made a mistake again. Why couldn't she be relaxed, she asked herself. Why couldn't she do what the others were doing?

"Well, Miss Teacher, I could tell. My name is Ben, at your service."

He bowed into the water, splashing her.

"Teacher, you have to get wet, really wet, in here," he said, mocking her.

"I thought we were exchanging names." She moved away a little, towards her haven of safety in the shallow end. "I am Pauline," she said, holding out her hand.

Ben was again laughing uproariously. "The Jamaican water is nice," he said, mercilessly pulling her under and causing her to come up spluttering.

"No," she said, pulling away as her eyes burned.

"I won't do that again but next time you will go under freely. Watch..."

And so, the lesson began and continued in the sea, after morning sharing and lunch. By then, she was a little more comfortable, though not willing to take any risks.

"Ben, please do not leave me out here. This is so far." She was protesting after she realized that they were right by the buoys marking their limit.

But Ben fully intended to let her try, so he swam away towards the rest of the party which had maintained a more conservative distance.

She was alarmed at being so far from the others, although the water was just at her waist, and to make things worse, a long wave was moving forward. She did not want to look silly but she did not want to drown.

But Ben had come swiftly back. "Do you know you could have screamed, instead of looking so terrified? I'll show you the picture someone just took."

She was so relieved, she could not help smiling. He helped her back to the gleeful group, now busy with sand packing, foot printing, splashing others and any other prankish acts they could find.

Later, the evening was mellow as they sang by the bonfire: "If you miss the train I am on, then you know that I am gone, more than five hundred miles away from home." Local songs were great entertainment as the visitors would not give up on learning the language of their hosts.

Pauline suddenly wanted to stretch the three days into four, five, or even seven. No one wanted to go to bed but with all that sea water and frolicking around, they were tired and needed to start on time in order to complete the scheduled activities.

Breakfast was a sobering affair for her. She had made friends. She had gone beyond her boundary. She had stopped feeling lonely. She sat with Ben, Dianne and two others at the table. She encouraged them to try real local food. The chefs produced the most tempting dishes from various cultures, but some people did not find any appeal in strange foods. Nevertheless, Ben responded to Pauline's promoting, tried some local fruits, and was just bowled over.

"Teacher did that," said Ben. "She is almost as good a teacher as her teacher."

"Where did you learn that riddle?" Dianne asked, looking in amusement at Pauline. "Look what your teacher has brought out."

It was a quick meal because they had the final formal presentation sessions on discipleship. This was followed by discussion and group work, and presentations by each group.

Pauline was surprised that she was appointed group reporter and enjoyed the warm applause which followed her presentation.

It was surreal for Pauline. She did not know this new personality. It was as though she had known these persons for a long time and she went so far as to try to remember everyone's name.

The social at the end of the retreat filled her with the same sadness as it seemed to have done for everybody. They could have stayed forever. As she looked around at all the faces, she wondered where her early feelings of rejection had come from. Her eyes met Ben's and she knew the answer. Here was a friend who pulled her out of her shell and helped her to see her life through new lenses.

Oh, Aldine!

There it was, the sign I had spent the last forty minutes looking for, Lacy Drive. I paused for several seconds as though trying to interpret what was really a very prosaic name written on a normal rectangular metal strip and in its proper place to indicate the road. The scheme was at the end of the drive, and I proceeded along its short distance in great uncertainty to the end where I turned left as I had been bidden. My hesitancy grew as I parked along the perimeter wall facing the long row of apartments and separating the scheme from a neighbouring community.

As I disembarked, I could not help but notice the untidy settlement behind the wall with houses in various stages of completion, roofs secured by scattered blocks and overlaid with junk of all sorts. And the throbbing noise of what was supposed to be music assailed my unwilling ears.

I noted that my destination was a typical lower middle-income apartment complex. It featured clean surroundings, a grassy centre within the semi-circle of two-storey houses, many of which looked somewhat drab. But there were others that sported brightly coloured walls and grilles, and attractive gardens in the small, enclosed yard space they had. The few vehicles in the parking lot were characteristic of a complex in that bracket — an old model

Corolla, a Nissan sedan, a station wagon and an old, propped-up Hiace van without wheels leaning against the separating wall between the scheme and the adjoining settlement.

I could not believe that these were the circumstances in which Aldine lived now, a far cry from the community in which she was known to have lived. I remembered how, a few times, out of curiosity, I had just driven through that area en route to my friend's house farther on. My friend was always amused at the wonder with which I spoke of the community.

"You mean you came off the shorter main road to go through Sky View!"

"Well, that's all I can do," I had responded, finding it a bit amusing myself.

"My dear, I keep my head straight, no need to dazzle my eyes," she said. "My glimpse from the main is enough."

"Well, you ought to see the houses closer... cultured hedges, lawns so green they seem unreal and the cars – I'm sure that as soon as the residents saw mine, they knew I did not belong."

"And be sure not to linger in any suspicious-looking way or you should see the patrol car following very shortly."

The thought was amusing, but this was one such community.

We girls first met at St John's University. Although Aldine displayed very uptown middle-class attitudes, Judith and I from humbler backgrounds knew how to relate to her because underneath it all, she was a friendly person. The three of us would be strolling together on a Friday evening, and out of the blue Aldine would say, "Darlings, I am bored. How about a movie?"

"Aldine, my funds do not allow two movie weekends in a row," I would answer.

"No worries," she would say. "I don't mind sponsoring you guys."

Judith and I would look knowingly at each other. This was always a treat.

Other times we would go partying with our male friends. We would joke about our funny relationship with the fellows. There was no intimate relationship, but the three young men seemed to enjoy our company and always made themselves available. "Are we going any further with these very attentive guys?" I asked on our return from a party. That was after noticing how close Aldine had been with Jeffrey. Anyone looking on would have thought they were a serious item. "Oh, I think they are just good friends," Judith said.

"But they are nice people," I returned, knowing fully well that that would continue to be a nonargument.

"Listen my friends, Jerome is nice and helpful, and we do benefit from his car seeing that it's the only one in the group. No, Judith, we are not using him. That's what friends are for. Jeffrey is intellectually very stimulating, and I guess you notice that we enjoy arguing with each other. Alan is the quiet, sheepish one who would make a solid companion to someone," Aldine declared.

I thought they did more than argue at that party but kept my big mouth closed.

"So?" Judith pressed.

"So, let's enjoy their company and leave the future to take care of itself. . . but should I be speaking for either of you?" Aldine looked at us curiously.

"Maybe you have," I said, not caring.

"Leave all to time," Judith conceded.

Knowing Judith, I was not sure she had really rested the matter though.

After university, Aldine and I became colleagues in the same business. I was a supervisor in the company which supplied equipment to the health agency in which Aldine worked. She was a manager and married to a senior official in a related agency. We continued the friendship started in university, but I was conscious of her changing personality and cautioned by the snide remarks from her colleagues about her ruthlessness in the office. Reportedly, she was determined to have her own way, challenging even the leadership of the company.

It was difficult for me to imagine Aldine morphing into the monster portrayed in the reports, but it was even more challenging to picture Aldine living in the circumstances reported. The dissonance between the character I had known and the one I was anticipating, filled me with uncertainty as to what the visit would be like.

The number of the house hung prominently on a round metal

sign at the top of the door. I studied the number for a while, trying to come to terms with the fact that I had arrived. The sign, which seemed to have been painted green at some time, hung over an unkempt little square of a veranda with dirty lounge chairs and floors so discoloured that I could not imagine them ever being restored to what seemed to have been originally a beige colour. Ugly, cracked flower pots containing only caked-up soil stood haphazardly among the chairs. The thirsty soil, glazed with a greenish white film which could have been a fungus, had not even a hint of flowers. I looked at the front of the other apartments. Some boasted neat gardens and fencing while too many others struggled with coarse, unkempt grass.

I quickly recalled my reason for making this twenty-mile journey from out of town and moved towards the door. But as I stepped closer and raised my hand to knock, a whiff of the most fetid air that could be imagined met my nostrils. It was a surprising welcome. I turned swiftly to prevent my unruly nostrils from giving in to the involuntary need to inhale. The encounter caused me to question my reason for coming and that was a good thing because otherwise I would have been on my way in five minutes. I held my breath and knocked. For several moments, the disturbing smell was my only company and I kept turning my face outward between my not too gentle tapping to get fresh air. I kept knocking, expecting a response because I had been advised that Aldine was only at home before twelve. Other than that, I would have to see her after ten in the night, an option I was not prepared to take.

Several times, I turned to go as I could not become accustomed to the horrible scent, and I needed to accomplish that if I were to speak to her. Inhaling the sick odour on a continuous basis was just not possible and I stepped back a few feet from the door where I could drink my fill of fresher air.

After a refreshing five or so minutes, I valiantly stepped back into position and resolutely raised my hand and started to rap sharply on the door. Most of the windows around the quadrangle were closed, which gave me such a sense of freedom that I even stood on tiptoes to peep through Aldine's half-opened bedroom window. The silence of the place was disconcerting, and I felt a little nervous when there was a sudden movement of the curtains in the open window of a house on the second storey of the adjacent block. It was like a flash of light, almost an illusion; I soon began to think that it was only the result of the ongoing quivering caused by the wind.

I was ill prepared for the shuffling of feet which drew closer and closer to the door. I held my breath and waited, feeling momentarily as though any creature could appear. As the door opened, a rush of strong, putrid scent greeted me seconds before a woman, almost too changed for me to remember, appeared. This woman was oh so bedraggled, in a soiled, washed-out garment that hung loosely about her meagre frame. She was as thin as a broomstick and seemed to be about to topple. Maybe that was why she held on to the door jamb, I thought, not sure of my next action. I watched her every move, from the loose wobbly movement of her legs, to the clutching of the door with skinny hands, to the raising of a long, distressed, wrinkled face, with dull eyes crowned by bushy eyebrows as grey as the thinning crop of hair on her head.

She looked intently at me as she moved towards me, now standing as stiff as a board. I could not find what to say so I did not try. Then the glazed eyes opened wide, and she ejected a funny sound, more like a gasp, as she slowly leaned forward, dragging her left leg to join the other so she could straighten up.

"Janet? My God, what a surprise!" exclaimed the woman, her eyes rolling from my neatly locked and slightly greying straightened hair to my pretty, casual shift ending just below the knee, and to my flat expensive-looking black shoes. It was a little uncomfortable for me as I was not sure she was making a mental comparison. I was not sure at all.

"Aldine!" I said, carefully picking my words. "Such a long time."

I wanted to say much more but politeness held me back. I was unsure of what would be permissible.

Aldine was beaming.

"Well it's not my time to get up but since you are already here and I am already up, you may as well come in." She stepped aside to allow me in, but I was now almost suffocating from the overpowering scent.

Jesus, I thought. What on earth...? Curious, I slowly followed Aldine, who was busy lifting a pile of crumpled clothing, old newspapers, books, magazines, and a host of other things from a chair and transferring them to the top of a closed carton box which was on the floor. My frightened eyes raked through the muck on the table: dishes, pans, dirty table towels and empty soda bottles created an unholy clutter. Beyond that was the kitchen, a modern concept separated from the living area by a brief counter, with its own clutter. It was a major puzzle to sort the scattered utensils on the counter — soiled-looking pots, dishes, everything ever used in the kitchen and dining room — were represented on the surface in those spaces.

"So sit down nuh," Aldine's voice intruded on my confused mind. Quite oblivious to the unbelieving stare of her visitor, she seemed satisfied that she had made the place "comfortable" and was deserving of her own seat now.

Again, she beckoned to me, eager for the chit chat. "You are not going to stand, are you? Sit, Judith," she said, sounding a little impatient and imperious.

"Aldine dear, this is Janet," I corrected.

"Oh yes, so sorry. You are Janet. It's the damn memory..." Her flippancy belied the glib apology.

I had no choice, although I wavered as I saw the true state of the chair she was offering. My hesitancy was not just because of the sagging seat and plain blue upholstery that was torn in several places, but the discernible dirty spots scattered all over the surface, were very disconcerting.

"This is a pleasant surprise, one I've not had in a decade. Tell me what you have been doing," said Aldine, almost as engaging as she had been forty years ago in college. She had not lost her cultured and easy way of speaking. It was as though the words just rolled off her tongue. Lonesome souls in the mess that surrounded them, they stood out, in sharp contrast, from the reality of the situation. I knew I had to speak, that I would be forcing every word, but she did not notice my struggle. She was smiling in anticipation as she led the way and sat in the emaciated, suspicious-looking couch.

"I am running my own business now. I live in America and came to visit my parents. I thought of catching up with you and so did some enquiries," I said, trying to peep at the bedroom. I could not say what my little research had yielded but she had been anything but a fool at any time in her life.

"Yes, how did you find me? This is interesting. How long has it been since university? Have you seen any others? Maureen was one of our circle, wasn't she? " I concentrated hard on the volley of questions, opting for the ones I could answer. "Oh yes, and Judith. Hear she actually married Alan..." She seemed incredulous.

"Yes, so she told me, but we were not in touch at the time. None of us three were in touch." I knew Maureen had not been "one of the group" but had no wish to prolong the conversation.

Breathing was difficult; I could not hold my breath for several minutes at a time.

"I am in touch with a few persons. Remember Pauline? She is in New Jersey with her family. Maureen is here somewhere. I need to find her. So this is how it is, we are in our different corners."

This was unbelievable. I had to leave before I needed the bathroom, I thought in panic. I just did not want to imagine it. "Remind me what business you are in," continued Aldine, her eyes dancing with pleasure at seeing her long-time friend.

"Oh, I am actually a lawyer and I run my own little concern," I offered as matter-of-factly as I could.

"What!" exclaimed Aldine, the 't' echoing for emphasis. "I may need you."

This must be a joke, I thought. But I could not tell with a mind so disconnected from reality. I chuckled. "I am sure with your popularity and your educational background, you can find any number of lawyers."

"My dear, lawyers cost money. Even you," she said, teasing me. She had always been one for sarcastic humour and I could not decide whether she was serious or not, and I really did not want to probe. I felt like a robot. I found things to say, nice things that would not cause any discomfort. Finally, I asked, "Did you complete your masters?" Then wished I could retract the question the minute the last word fell.

"I almost did but had a spot of problem, and decided that the resources could not stretch. But I would go back now if I got help. The pension alone could not do it," she said, looking at me as though she needed my opinion.

You're kidding, I thought. Aldine, you are out of it.

"Where do you live now?" she asked, taking me by surprise.

"Well, I did say I live in the States," I answered, a visible look of confusion on my face. "You forgot that I just said that?"

"My dear, my short-term memory is bad. It's just one of those things," she said as though she said that every day.

Short term indeed, I mused inwardly.

I could not find anything to contribute, so I moved on.

"Well, studying is always an option, at any age," I said, feeling like a true hypocrite. My lungs now felt as if they would burst. I wanted to go. I am going to be out of here in the shortest possible time, I thought, in a few moments, if I can survive that much. In the meantime, I would have to talk, somehow. But Aldine helped by picking up. 'The old talker', I remembered fondly and I felt as though the chaos of my friend's life was a tangible thing that was sitting on my head. My eyes grew moist and I was as choked up from the sadness as I was from the unbearable smell.

Aldine saw that something was wrong and stopped prattling to ask, "You okay, Judith?" Then, at the escape of a violent cough, she said, "Some water would be good. Sorry, there is no ice, but even tap water is good, even better they say; but you know how we are, not really caring as long as we get what's nice."

I wanted to cry now when I heard the sharp comments and the logic of the reasoning. She had risen from the chair and was moving slowly towards the fridge. I did not want her to get the water, so I acted quickly. I responded to my stressors and rose suddenly to go, which caused her to retrace her steps. "You are not having the water? I don't want my guest to be uncomfortable at all. That's not me. That's one of the things my mother, bless her soul, taught me."

"I am okay. It's time for me to leave anyway. Have to make a stop on the way home." I was turning as I spoke.

"Where do you work? You must be in one of those big companies in the city."

"Oh," I tried to be rather off-hand. "I have my own law office in Miami. I don't live in Kingston. Have not lived in Jamaica for over thirty years." I had started carefully controlled steps towards the door, and she was right behind me. At the door, I paused to allow her to open it.

"You are as forgetful as I am. It must be the ageing thing. Weren't we basically the same age?" she asked, searching my face.

"About," I remembered.

As I stepped outside, she pointed out as though for the first time, "My short-term memory is really bad. Just have to live with that. Can't do much about ageing, can we?" She smiled and I knew the visit had been good for her, memory or not.

"Aldine," I said, hugging her, really hugging her. "I am going. I'll not leave for another two weeks so you will see me again."

As she stepped through the door, a woman passed and turned in surprise at seeing me.

"Oh, she have visitor?" she asked, looking at me in disbelief. "You her relative?' she asked, giving Aldine a dirty look.

"What do you want?" Aldine asked, pulling her bad leg alongside the good one. "Leave me alone."

"I leave you alone when you clean up the place," the lady said, her voice climbing a couple of decibels.

"Okay, can we not have an argument?" I ventured timidly, not wanting to see Aldine upset.

"What the hell you troubling me for? I live with you?" Aldine's voice was also lifting.

"You are a nasty woman. You must move."

"Nasty like your damn nasty pickney them?" Aldine's dam broke and let loose a flood of the worst words. And she was talking to the whole complex. I did not know what to do. How could she live like this? The woman was satisfied she had given me the picture and she wheeled her tall, slim, slightly bent body and continued along the pathway, calling Aldine all sorts of names and obviously seeking endorsement from two ladies who had come out of their houses. I was glad they merely looked on, but I suspected that was out of deference for me as a visitor.

I turned to Aldine, who had now calmed down. Again, I was puzzled. She seemed spent and just stood there saying nothing. I suspected that in another ten minutes she would have forgotten this incident.

I made a grand display of patting her on the back and hugging her. Then I invited her to walk me to the car and promised loudly to call again soon. I meant it but I did not know how I would be able to relive this experience.

To the Unknown Herb

In the kitchen, Edith tried to focus on the details of her dish- washing as the means of blocking the disturbing sound of George's moaning in the bedroom. She felt a little self-conscious about closing the kitchen door but that was what she wanted to do. It was another of those nights for her. George was suffering this inexplicable pain that kept her plying a clearly defined route from the bedroom to the living room to the kitchen, all in her effort to find a remedy that worked. The expected call came breathless, loud and demanding. "Edith, where the medicine from Dr Thomas? Bring it nuh. Bring it nuh. Lawd. Lawd. Whoi."

"Coming, George. Jus' hol' on nuh man. A coming."

Edith always thought that at these times George lost all sense of reason. She could not figure out why he always overdid things. She had felt so much pain in her life. She had suffered, delivering the two children now adults and away in America, one with induced labour and the other, a caesarean section. She also recalled a broken leg which she sustained on her way to the river one morning when she slipped on a stone and hurtled like a well-tuned roller coaster down the hill. And there were many other times when she felt terrible pain but she did not go on like that. All the same, she reasoned, man don't bear pain well. With all the talk and the big boast, them weak like rat, she thought with a chuckle.

"Edith, come nuh. You don't know man sick. Man sick, Edith, come." His voice took on a whining tone.

"I know man dead sometimes!" shouted Edith, pushing her head through the door to make sure he heard.

"You is a wicked woman!" he shouted back with all his strength. "Can't even ..." but the persistent pain returned just like labour pains, intermittent and consuming, and he was forced to refocus his attention.

It was not that Edith was not concerned and would not like to help, but she did not know what to do. Dr Thomas would not be in his office now so they would have to wait until the next day or take the long hours waiting at the public hospital. She wished nothing worst happened. After forty-five years of life with George, she could not bear it. And worse of all, Sandy and Sammy were so far away. They called from time to time to enquire about their father's health and regularly sent money to help with the expenses, but that was all they could do.

"George, I comin'. You not goin' to dead. A just joking. Doh worry." She walked as briskly as she could into the room, carefully carrying a hot cup of green tea on the little plastic tray which she placed on the bedside table. The steam rose wistfully into the warm air of the room which had all the windows drawn to confine the sounds of distress. George, a fifty-eight year old, greying black man, raised painfully on his shaking elbow, groaning loudly. His bushy beard moved in time with each huge bellow, and he alternated between sitting up and reclining quickly in agony, wrinkling his already furrowed face in exasperation.

"Woman, han' me the tea, nuh," he expelled in mounting annoyance.

"All right," she said in eager compliance, "mine you burn up you'self." With that she gently raised the cup, and obviously changing her mind, said, "Try sit up. Let me feed you." She was stooping over him, and he wistfully sniffed her sweet-scented talc as though it offered some balm. After carefully taking a tentative sip, he raised his grey clouded eyes in appreciation of her help and then hesitantly opened his mouth to receive slightly larger amounts. He took a few swallows, each one so slow that Edith thought this was her night's work. "It too hot," he offered apologetically. "A trying to drink it quick. A need to drink it quick."

"You can't go quick yet. You said I was to make it hot but is alright. Take your time. I not in any hurry." He looked curiously at her, noting her great effort at being patient. Her tone did not match her slightly pouting mouth. But soon he was turning his back on her to deal with the pain. Edith stood, her lips tightly pursed in her mental search for answers. No sir, something must be done. "Let me rub you with some bay rum or Kananga water," she offered as she went uncertainly to the huge mahogany dressing table which kept most of their personal items. She brought the healing oil which she held aloft until he had raised the shirt of the blue striped pyjamas which he wore. He looked impatiently up at her, squeezing his stomach with both hands as if he was carefully kneading dough.

"Mista, I mus' rub you belly or not?" she asked when she felt the slight pressure of his hand as he tried to push her hand away. She knew she was not sounding very sympathetic to him, and she felt badly about this. She turned slightly towards the door. "You goin' on as if a doh have feelings, like is not pain a feeling." A small smile in the corners of her mouth did not show great empathy but she went closer and bending over him, she generously spread the liquid on her palms before resting the bottle on the pillow and rubbing his belly lavishly.

"Dat nuh help much," he said after a few minutes of her gentle but thorough ministration, his eyes pleading, "but thanks." He was back to the crying now almost as though he welcomed it. It did not take the pain away, but it gave him a little comfort. She was determined to seek help tonight. He would not know the depths of her sympathy for him. Probably she did not show it because he got on her nerves sometimes with his contradictory demands, but in her heart she felt his pain and wanted to find a means of relief. "Soon come, George," she threw at him and without waiting for an answer, she went quickly through the open front door towards the gate. She felt very conscious that he would be alone, but it did not make sense just giving him tea and massages.

Mr Hibbert was seated on his veranda when she arrived at his gate. He was renowned for his knowledge of herbs which he shared willingly with his neighbours and even people from farther afield. In true country style, some persons quietly harboured the notion that he was really a 'Do-Good Man', but he would not entertain that notion when anyone ventured to say that. However, that was as far as they would go because he did not call on spirits nor use oils and scents. He merely dispensed herbs and advice. "The herbs of the field are for our healing — so the good book say." He always ended with those words to emphasise the authenticity of his approach.

"Who is there?" he asked. "Remember the old man half bline yuh know. So yuh have to talk up." He had raised himself from the wooden reclining chair and was standing at the gate of the veranda, waiting for his visitor to declare himself.

"Mr Hibby, is me Edith. George take down again with the belly and a caa fine a way to help. O lawd, poor George. Him really sufferin'."

He swung the veranda gate open and came towards the yard gate. At sixty-eight Cecil Hibbert was as strong as an ox. He was tall and imposing, and just slightly stooping. He came to her, resting his elbow on the column at the gate and conveying genuine sympathy from his grey eyes to his furrowed face. "Tell me exactly what happenin' to ma frien'," he invited.

As she spoke, he rubbed the front of his thinning greying hair continuously in slow motion, listening in deep contemplation. When he was satisfied with the amount of information he had been given, he turned slightly towards the house, his brow knitted. Then he came back to her, opening the gate. As he led her round the side of the house towards the back, he said, "Miss Edith, Miss Gem not here. You know is her church night and should be mine too but maybe it jus' too late for the ole man. Poor Gem trying to get me there for over thirty years since she start goin'."

Edith chuckled, fully aware of the frustration felt by her friend. Sometimes, she could not withhold her amusement at the pranks Gem recounted that were played by Mr Hibbert and all were intended to show that he was unable to go to church at a particular time. She did not know if he had even been to church twelve times over the forty-five years of their marriage. She recalled the time when Gem had carefully planned an invitation to a Christmas cantata where his grandniece would be performing. Now Gem thought she could play on his unfailing love for his niece and her family, and it was with some confidence that she brought the lovely, crafted invitation which outlined a programme bearing the names of all the performers. Gem said she became very hopeful when her husband read the programme with interest and promised to look into the matter. But the following morning, he started displaying shortness of breath which he declared to be very uncomfortable. As a result, he stayed in bed and declined to eat breakfast. All he took was a little tea. Gem had been incredulous.

"Mr Hibby, where you get short o' breath from?"

"Dear, a doh know how it come upon me so. A not anxious over nothin," he said with his chest heaving rapidly and his face screwed up seemingly in the effort to get enough breath.

" Well," said Gem, "hope you get better by evening cause Trudy said you have to come to see Sara perform or none of them will forgive you."

"A hope so too, Gem," he had replied. "I really want to see my little dawlin on stage." If Gem detected a note of mockery, she was going to pretend she did not and waited to see what would happen. So, she went through her day's activities, checking on him at intervals. At about two-thirty, he announced that he needed to go to the doctor and asked for her help to put him together. She felt sorry for him, now thinking that she had misjudged him.

"A really sorry a not goin' to see ma pumkin, ma little pumkin," he said as he picked up his bag, packed just in case he had to stay over.

"Well, yuh cyaan do any better, Mr Hibby. Is not you call sickness so Trudy and Sara understan'."

He turned left at the gate to get a taxi at the corner about ten chains from the house. Poor Gem was so sad that she had not gone with him but he had insisted that he was not dying so he would be able to manage. Well, she would soon find out that he was certainly far from dying. By the time she was leaving for the cantata three hours later, she started sniffling and felt she might not make it but the thought of Sara not seeing both of them was enough to push her out. So, she went in the direction he had gone which was opposite to where she normally travelled to get some flu tablets from the nearest shop.

A great racket greeted her as she entered. It came from the playing of dominoes in what was used as a sports room by the men of the community, especially the domino players. And it was a raucous game in progress with shouts of victory or annoyance, and words that caused her to want to plug her ears with something hard. She had bought her tablets and was turning to leave when she picked out a clear voice of disappointment.

"Mr Hibby, yuh lock me down man. Cho Mr Hibby."

"Not my fault, Rory. Watch the game, man."

Gem stood stock still with her outstretched arm in mid-air. No, she thought, he mus' be comin' from doctor. But no, she thought again, he should not be back so soon. Allowing an hour and a half for travelling and at least two hours waiting time at the doctor, he should not be here now. She had no doubt he had again lamped her. But she reasoned, since he preferred hell, it was okay.

"Now, Miss Edith, a caa see well so you have to follow ma guidance," Mr Hibby was saying. "You looking fo' a bush that kill any pain. It is the greatest. It name Puss Ears. Now a trying to fine it but you mus' help me."

He moved deftly among the luxurious growth of vegetables, fruits and herbs occupying about three squares of gently sloping land at the rear of the house. The playful evening breeze kept the plants shivering busily with their continuous whisper of appreciation. "A know that what a lookin' for is to the side here but although the outside light shining a not so sure. Let a look some more. " He led a trail along the fence using almost all his senses to verify which plant he was searching for.

"I doh know it Mr Hibby but I hear people say it good."

"Yes, aah! A think this is it — caa quite tell the colour green but the leaf is the right size and the edge have some little things like bristle and it feel like velvet. Jus' tell me the exac' colour green. Mus' be sure cause all kind o' bush grow among the good plants — what the good book say? Wheat and tares mus' grow together." He laughed mirthfully knowing that Gem hated when he quoted the Bible but never showed interest in church.

"You sure, Mr Hibby. I know you is our doctor for the herbs but we can't make any mistake."

"Miss Edith. A think we have it." He held a small sprig of green bush in his hand. He ran his fingers over it. He smelled it. "Is it, Ms Edith. Just use about seven leaves, an' draw them, don't boil them. Okay ma'am?"

"Mr Hibby, God bless. I hurrying home to the gentleman. "

"Tell him to obey you and watch see what happen."

"Tomorrow, Mr Hibby. God bless you." She could not wait to go through the gate. Lord, she could only imagine George how he would be wringing hand, foot and everything.

And sure enough, George was in a tizzy. The howling was loud from the gate and as she dashed inside thinking he was worse, he shouted, "A woman leave her sick husban' and gone to chat! A think a have to go to the doctor!"

"George, I get something good from Mr Hibby. Is a wonder herb."

"Mine what you give me, woman. Mine you kill me," he cautioned.

But Edith was paying him no attention. The pot was already on and in five minutes, there was enough hot water to make the first cup. She poured the liquid between cups, watching the steam escape with each pour. At last it was cool enough and she hurried in to George.

He was broken and compliant. Not a word was said as he obediently drank the liquid and lay back against the pillows. Edith pretended not to show any fear. She took the cup out and washed it. Then as she puttered around the kitchen, she heard the groans. But somehow, she sensed or heard a softening of the sounds. It was slight but unmistakeable. She went in quietly, saying nothing. It was George who spoke.

"Edith, a feel a little ease. Jeese!"

"Aah, George. I am glad. Make we watch some more."

She moved the only chair in the room from before the window to the bedside so she could watch him. The groaning grew lower and farther apart until she noticed he was getting sleepy. "Oh praise the Lord!" she shouted as he went off to sleep. "Bless Mr Hibby, Father. Him bring relief to my husband and me. Bless him for me. We can sleep tonight."

And she slept. They both slept and in the same room that night. In the morning, both of them expressed incredibility at what had happened. George got up to do his usual chores before having breakfast which his wife fixed with euphoric anticipation. They had just been seated at the table when they heard the frantic knocking on the gate. Edith checked to see Mr Hibbert there. His long nose was glistening from the brisk walk he had undertaken to get to their house.

"Mr Hibby, what happen?" she asked, noting his agitated state.

"Let me in. A need to see George. We have to get him to the doctor now!"

"But why, Mr Hibby? You doh hear how the house quiet. George not groaning and waking up the neighbours. You doh notice?"

"But Miss Edith. A think is a bad bush George get. When a check this morning is a strange bush a give you." With that he took a little paper bag from his pocket and pulled out a sprig of bush. At first glance it seemed just like the one he had given her, but when he pulled out the piece of the first one, the difference was clear. Both were small and soft with serrated edges, but the bush he intended was a lighter green and had a longer tip. Mr Hibbert was so distressed, he could not stand still.

"What's happening out there?" George asked, coming towards them. "Oh, Mr Hibby; God bless you! We both goin' to church after this. You miracle bush work like magic!"

"George, you not dying? You not dying or dead?"

"A not a duppy," said George, using the most nasal tone he could find. Then he said in his normal voice, "Why? You think something wrong?"

The explanation had George erupting in uproarious laughter as loud as the noises he emitted during his ordeal. "So, you come to bury me? You is a real good frien'," he said, shaking with laughter. He beckoned Mr Hibbert closer. "Touch me and see if me real or me is a duppy," he said between loud guffaws.

But Mr Hibbert did not need that proof. Edith joined them and the three went into the house. In the dining room, they chattered like children about the miracle bush, while Edith served chocolate tea and fried dumplings with salted mackerel.

"We goin' to name this bush that heal me miracle bush, and a planting some today, Hibby. Beg you give me a plant," sputtered George between guffaws of laughter. When Mr Hibbert rose to go, he was still laughing and swaying like a slender tree exposed to a strong wind. "Let me go home. A caa bear this shock. A never see that bush in my life, the miracle bush. It jus' spring up."

George was still laughing. "Is God sen' it fo' me." He raised his eyes above.

Mr Hibbert was still looking in wonder. "You better go to church Georgie bwoy."

Then George said, "Yuh comin' if a live until morning? Mr Hibby, thank you..."

"I won't be sure until I wake up tomorrow morning and you still okay," Mr Hibbert said, trying to sound a little cautious.

"Cho man, you can sleep sound. Tonight, about eight o'clock will be twenty-four hours." George watched him go through the gate before returning to his home. Edith followed her husband inside.

"George, tomorrow morning you must pay him a visit," she said, feeling certain that she herself would be having another very restful night. "But careful, he might still think you are a duppy."

"Thank the good Lord for the miracle bush," she said quietly to herself.

Going To Father

It was not yet dawn when the two women and the little twelve-year old girl scurried through the back door of the house in a routine the girl had experienced for as long as she could remember. With hurried nervous care, her mother closed the door, and as they descended the track behind the house, they kept glancing furtively to the right where Maas Abe might be working on the farm. It had been to their utter dismay that Maas Abe had positioned his new block and steel house farther back from the road, and therefore lower down the slope than the first one. He was now slightly behind them.

The two women and the little girl lived in a little three-apartment board house consisting of a hall and two bedrooms. The bathroom and the kitchen were outside the house. On their three-acre hillside plot, they farmed cash crops in the tradition of the agrarian lifestyle of the community. They were decent people and they were not troubling anyone. The women were good people who could never understand why their enemies should "take set on them". The child was doing well in school and the family abroad were doing well.

Every now and then, a big carton, well taped, with large, brightly coloured scrawling, wide-spaced letters made with markers, would come through the post office. The nosy people could only imagine what was in it and every time, the children were told not to wear what they got immediately. Let the nosy people wait. Every now and then too, an airmail letter would come with its bright slanted stripes and black markings and stamps and stickers that squealed "foreign". The mother did not like to collect the letters when certain people were in the post office, so if she went and saw them there or they came in and saw her there, she would find some excuse to go elsewhere and return later.

The old man and his wife had lived on the neighbouring five acres of land for as long as Rachel and her parents had occupied their property. It had been a relatively peaceful coexistence, though not without the occasional disagreement over their chickens scratching his vegetables or his cutting of a tree that they felt was on their side of the line. However, on no occasion did the discord result in long-term damage. And none lasted beyond Christmas when the village was transformed into one big family.

Last Christmas, their family and Maas Abe's, buried another hatchet from early morning when the bursting of the firecrackers started.

Maas Abe had shouted, "Miss Angie, look like you buy out all of Miss Maud shop!"

Rachel's mother, who seemed to get an enormous high out of discharging the explosives, responded, "Boy, Maas Abe, is my little fun dis," and she giggled gleefully. This was one of the few times Rachel had heard her laugh without restraint.

Maas Abe let out a huge whoop and drawing closer, he cautioned her.

"A young pretty woman like you can have better fun." She was a little discomfited by the remark and could see that her mother was too. Many times, Rachel had seen him looking across the fence and had suspected it was in her mother's direction, even when his wife was outside helping him on the farm. But Rachel saw that, even while being polite, her mother was not going to encourage the conversation.

"Rachie and me goin' in now so we can eat and get ready," her mother said.

He chuckled.

Her father's unforgiveable departure from the home three years ago had not quenched the love of Rachel's mother and grandmother for church. In addition, her mother and grandmother insisted that she should go every Sunday even when they were unable to.

"Pray fo' me and the old lady, " Maas Abe returned. She was sure that this was a request he kept repeating solely for the purpose of teasing her. He did not have a religious bone in his body.

"Miss Susie! Miss Susie!" Rachel's mother called out to her grandmother who was busy cooking inside. Rachel did not miss the intention in that.

Rachel had been unprepared for her parents' sudden declaration the night before that they would be going to "look after their life" the following morning. Rachel knew immediately what that meant. She knew they had not involved her, firstly, since she was a child, and secondly, because she hated those trips.

With well-practised care, they headed down the hill, intending to take an obscure path to the main road. Going by the northerly road would not only have taken them higher up in the village but would have attracted much more attention and aroused the suspicion of the village that they should be leaving at that time, and on a Sunday when they would have been normally preparing for church. People in the village who went on long journeys on a Sunday always attracted suspicion and gossip.

They walked, hardly talking, using their knowledge of the bumpy, unpaved, parochial road to guide their harried steps. At first, the only other signs of life were the continuous murmuring of the distant birds housed in the canopies of the trees. But the comfortable feeling inspired by the calming sounds of birds and gently rustling leaves was suddenly pierced by an eerie, screeching sound reverberating across the valley. The women looked at each other and crossed themselves three times each. The *patoo* bird was the last thing they wanted to hear.

The girl's mother started to recite Psalm 27, "The Lord is my shepherd..." in an awful sonorous voice that spoke of fear and anxiety. In the cool morning, the pervasive mist absorbed the half-light, giving everything an ethereal appearance. As the darkness receded, the mist grew thicker, sometimes seeming to roll before them like a puff of dust disturbed by a deliberate broom. In voices muffled by fear, they traded well-worn stories about their neighbours, which brought much laughter to them but not to the girl, who just trod heavily along.

When day broke, they should be at the train station where they could melt into the anonymity of strangers. The women always felt relief when they reached this part of the journey. They had left their troubles behind for a day and could look back dispassionately at the village. Even their worst enemies did not seem threatening from this distance. Everyone would be just waiting. Sometimes Rachel identified someone's destination by their clothing, usually a travel bag or handbag told her nothing. But Rachel's greatest interest was her morning tea which she knew was packed in one of the large calico bags they carried. Her mother had that. She wanted the food very badly and was just waiting for them to reach a spot where they could stop. She knew what was in the food bag — a large thermos of mint tea, thick buttered slices of bread in a plastic lunch box and fried salt fish in another container. They had also stacked plastic eating and drinking containers for all of them. All that had been done the night before.

By the time they boarded, the sun was peeping shyly from behind the hills, its soft yellow light not yet able to challenge the dew, spread possessively over the leaves, grass and other surfaces. Rachel enjoyed the rush of the wind as the train swept along on the plains, accompanied by the rhythmic clickety clack of the wheels on the track. She held her breath sometimes when the train swept along in what seemed like an uncontrolled motion. But it soon settled back into the former pattern of sound and movement.

Rachel wished the journey by train would never end. It was the only pleasant part of the experience. On the last occasion she had learnt another meaning of the word "mother". Today, her first encounter with the balm yard was an authoritative, spreading middle-aged woman dressed in an ugly, blue, long-sleeved dress, and wearing a red and blue headwrap. The long dress was trimmed with white at the cuffs and the collar, the wrap was twirled tightly around her head, and a red pencil rested rakishly in place behind her ear.

The woman was carrying out a tense and involved ceremony in the front of the yard. The centre of the ceremony was a table covered in a brilliant white tablecloth which reached down to the ground. Spread on the table were sprigs of leaf of life, three grapefruits, a bottle of cream soda, and in the centre, a white enamel bowl of water. A brass metal cross about two feet tall stood prominently in front of the arrangement.

The girl looked suspiciously at the scene as the woman circled a pliant young man with her huge bulk jiggling constantly. She chanted a song Rachel recognised as a revival song sung at street meetings and nine nights, as well as at the Pentecostal church she passed on Sundays. Her church sang more traditional hymns and songs. The Mother's large, heaving bosom was accompanied by equally timed grunts, betraying her energy level. But she did not pause as she executed the ritual. She twirled her black and yellow flag to describe all sorts of figures over the young man's head and around his body, and then sent him circling around the magic table. As though in a trance, he executed the moves she commanded, moving around the table, pausing to bow before the cross and then continuing around the full circle.

But Rachel did not have much time for contemplation because very shortly, a new participant, a slim, wiry woman, emerged from the side of the house. She was dressed in white from her high-necked long-sleeved blouse to her shoes. On her head she wore an intricately wrapped blue and red head dress, and her taut, long, bony face was somewhat averted. She waited disinterestedly until the dramatic ritual ended when the spinning lady dipped her hand in the bowl of water and made the dripping wet sign of a cross on the boy's forehead. Seemingly oblivious to the woman who conducted the ritual, the new lady briefly surveyed the visitors and then led the young man in the direction from which she had come.

The girl's mother felt rather than saw her stiffen and pull back. Lowering her eyes and avoiding the woman who stood waiting for them to come to her, the girl frantically glanced around the area and as if impelled by some devil, took a few steps back. The Mother stood waiting, her eyes lowered and her face wearing a scowl that reminded Rachel of nimbus clouds. The girl's grandmother noticed and became concerned. However, she was astute enough to quickly ease the tension by stepping quickly into place before the Mother. Ignoring her and her mother, the Mother proceeded to conduct the curious rite with the grandmother. As expected, her grandmother was also submissive and eager to please, and the Mother actually relaxed with her. And as expected, as soon as that session was completed, the thin woman appeared robot-like to lead her ward to the unknown destination.

Then Rachel's mother went forward to the woman, cautioning her not to move because it would be her turn next. Her mother circled nervously, afraid that she might be disobedient. The girl was nervous just watching her mother's initiation. She knew she had no power to avoid becoming part of this puzzle. She expected all sorts of magic and spirits that she had read about or had been told about in stories by her parents. She was relieved that her mother waited for her and asked the slim woman, when she came, to wait for her daughter. She seemed to have no difficulty granting the request, and as usual she stood uninvolved to the side, seeming to be focusing on other matters.

By the time Rachel was beckoned to the table, her body felt as stiff as a piece of board. Her legs felt as though they did not belong to her, and she had no control over them.

"Mother haul this little own way pickney, for me," the woman said, shaking her head in annoyance. "The spirit can't work with resistance. She mus' obey."

Holding her hand and propelling her forward, Rachel's mother whispered urgently, "Go quick. Don' make Mother leave the stand." The poor girl found herself looking fearfully up into the accusing eyes of the woman whose fat, shiny face was once again set in a frightening frown. Her mother had withdrawn as she thought she should and was watching anxiously from the side of the table.

With a sharp hiss, the woman took her hand. “Child you must do everything I say. Understand?”

The girl’s mind felt uneasy. *Everything?* was her silent question as she stole a glance at the woman.

As if reading her thoughts, the woman said impatiently, “I mean everything. Your mother can’t control you but doh bring it here. The spirit ready, girl! Don’t keep the Holy Spirit waiting.”

Ignoring the girl’s shivering, the woman stepped back and began chanting.

After this brief ceremony they passed through the yard — the wild rock gardens with plants bordered by whitewashed stones, and here and there a stand with a bowl of water and a grapefruit beside it. And the pigeons with their eerie flapping wings flying just anywhere they pleased or hopping about the yard on their scrawny little pink feet — the girl loved pigeons. Maas Simon reared a lot of pretty pigeons down the road from their house and she loved to shoo them and see them take flight, or to see them folding their wings as they alighted on a surface of their choice. But this time she was afraid of pigeons. These looked different. They reminded her of patoo birds which always made her afraid.

As if by relay, a busy-looking, small-bodied, youngish woman with a kindly face, met them at the next door through which they must pass. This would lead them to the church hall, the front entrance of which was surprisingly closed.

The hall was big, much bigger than the church at home. The altar sat at the far end of a larger platform bordered by a well-polished wooden rail which was draped with white curtains. Behind that was a wooden podium with a large, wooden bird, looking like an eagle in her reading book, as though it would fly into the audience any minute and peck the heck out of anyone it disliked. At the back of the platform was a fully curtained area which she knew to be where the pool was. Rachel saw the stained-glass windows on either side of the rear wall and hundreds of candles on tables below it. She could not count the colours. The candles were big and bulky and one row of them was lit, giving off a mix of sweet, terribly sweet odours. She looked cautiously around at the rows and rows of people who sat singing and rocking as though in pain. Their voices rose and swelled and drawled tunelessly on in songs that were generally familiar to her but sounded so awful she wanted to block her ears.

There were so many people attending this church and they were all dressed in the same colour. They all had head wraps, even the men. Rachel had never seen so many persons in a church. The air was charged and expectant and she grew afraid. She did not speak but allowed herself to be led to a bench where she sat between her mother and grandmother. The two women seemed pleased with their progress, but Rachel sat with her face straight and expressionless, not daring to show her annoyance that her parents did not seem to have any problem with just sitting and waiting because the singing was just to fill up time. It went on forever and she finally dulled her mind in the effort to endure it.

As the service progressed, a short, stocky man appeared at the door behind the altar. He had a noticeable paunch of which he seemed both conscious and proud. His large, round, balding head sat above a rough, puffy face and a mouth, which when opened revealed a row of far too even teeth dotted with glistening gold. He waited patiently for the collection plate and receiving it, looked askance at the contents. His face grew rigid as he turned to the congregation.

"The spirit tell me is only coins in the plate. You people think penny penny can run church?"

He strode across the platform while everyone sat in mesmerised silence.

"Well no church going on until real money in the plate, for is money run church."

Someone said, "Amen." And so the plate was once again passed around and money was soundlessly dropped into it. The mother and grandmother fetched their contribution from the knots on their bras. And the service went on as though by magic.

Sitting beside the two women, Rachel could feel their expectancy. Father was known to be good, reading up everything about his clients and prescribing just the right remedy.

"When we going to see the man?" asked Rachel after several songs, as she watched people in front disappearing slowly singly or in groups through the door to the right side of the platform.

"Shhh." Her mother spoke hastily. "Who you calling the man?" And she looked around at the nearby persons, concerned that someone might have heard. I would not mind, Rachel thought. I want him to run me out of here.

The congregants continued singing, rocking their now weary frames to the slow, solemn rhythm of the songs. Almost suddenly, they being now at the head of the line, were being sent to the door. Their usher, a thin, spindly, brown woman, somehow managed to convey a sense of the spiritual and the mysterious, and on entering the adjoining room, adopted a most pious and submissive demeanour.

A man was seated at a table in the centre of the room. His eyes were closed in meditation and he was wearing a bulky, red head wrap in a style she had seen before. He had covered his regular clothing with a long white robe which was brushing the floor as he sat, and there was a long, red band around his waist. It took some time to realise that this was the same man who had come into the church. She just kept looking at him trying to figure out if he was really the Father.

The two women sat reverently before the man who appeared to be unaware of them in the room. His huge, flabby lips were moving slightly, giving a glance every now and then of the shiny gold dots on his teeth. Vials of all shapes, colours and sizes rested on the shelf above the man's chair. And the walls were papered with pictures of Mary, of angels and lambs, and of the white-skinned blue-eyed Jesus looking in compassion at the piteous.

She did not realise when the Father became awake from his reverie, but now his eyes were wide open and he was assessing the family before him. In a surprisingly gentle voice, he asked, "What can I do for you, ladies? The big ladies and the little lady?" He looked at them with a wide smile. She did not know what to make of his approach.

Caught off guard, the women did not know how to respond. Finally, her mother ventured, "We want you to tell us about our life."

He chuckled as if he knew everything.

"What happening to yuh life? What happening is that all of you messed up by the enemy."

The women held their breath. They sat enthralled by the confirmation they were getting. They knew it. The girl waited with her brows wrinkled in curiosity. She knew from what her parents had brought back from such occasions that there was going to be somehow an interpretation of the enemy as the "long, meagre, long-faced black woman" who lived two doors away. But Father only said the same enemy they'd had for years was trying to hurt them. It was a good thing they had come early or else, "You woulda salt," he said to her mother, his eyes rolling towards heaven. But he could fix it. He would fix the wicked wretch and get her off them. If they wanted him to fix the problem, he would. But they indicated that they just wanted to protect themselves.

For that, he advised, they had to pay a little money, and then go to the drug store nearest to them and fortify themselves with the necessary oils and other protective stuff. They would have to burn incense in every room and sprinkle the holy water around the house and at the four-corner fence every night at exactly the same time.

"Wait, nobody can't write? You think you can remember all that I telling you?" he asked, annoyed.

"Don't you have a pen and a book? Write down everything," said the grandmother to Rachel's mother, recalling another occasion when they could not remember the name of one of the oils to buy.

For the follow-up trip they needed to bring two black pigeons or buy two from him. This was for the sacrifice.

They left satisfied, and marvelling about their timing. Once again they had forestalled the witch, that wicked, grudgeful wretch who had been trying to hurt them all these years. Yes, anywhere they were to get the money to pay Father, they would get it.

The girl listened in boredom as they walked from the bus to the house. At that late hour, she did not care. She was tired and hungry and wanted to reach inside. She would not be going next time, she had a plan! Suddenly her face brightened and she stepped so briskly that she was now ahead of her parents.

"Eh, eh!" her mother said. "Even Rachie feel better now. A tell you, you have to look out for yourself in this place. Nobody going to do that for you."

Her grandmother too, was very pleased.

"Wait for us chile. We just starting. We still have to find the money."

But something in her voice told Rachel that that would not be a real problem.

Colour Red

"What did you say, Marcy?" Aretha Abrahams asked her daughter. As usual, when they returned from the supermarket, they sat at the kitchen table for a few minutes before getting up to unload the groceries they had just taken from the car. One of them would put the kettle on for coffee, and a Danish or slice of cake or some other pastry. They would then have girl talk in the comfort of the cosy kitchen. This was a day when the helper was off, so they had the place to themselves. They were not in the habit of eating on the road while shopping.

Marcy busied herself making two steaming cups of coffee and preparing a slice of banana bread for each of them.

"Mom, I did not realise the picture had fallen from my bag. It's Hughie, a friend of mine." Marcy felt a sudden flush of fear.

"Friend from where?" Aretha demanded. She ignored the snack Marcy had placed on the table. "Hughie? Or is it, Hugh? Oh, I need the AC," she said, feeling faint. Through watery eyes she saw Marcy with grotesque features, bulging, spiteful eyes and twisted sneering mouth.

Marcy went swiftly to the switch, glad for the chance to escape the distress in her mother's face, if only for a minute.

Aretha looked at her daughter as though she did not know her. She was unable to find words enough to express her dismay. Friend? she asked herself. That does not look like a friend of my daughter's, she reasoned in her mind. A friend with pants hanging below the waist? What was she thinking, allowing me to see that horror?

"Mom . . ." Marcy hesitated, not knowing how to go on. Her mother rose to stand against the kitchen counter where she rested her back. She shook her head vigorously, her flying hair reflecting the confusion she was feeling. Suddenly, to Marcy, she seemed older than her fifty years. The lines underlining her eyes as well as those in her forehead seemed more prominent in that moment. The fear she was feeling seemed to overcome her and she appeared so tired she could only sit.

It was definitely not a good time for her father to come in.

"Arrie, you feeling sick?" he asked, as he walked quickly to his wife.

Marcy pretended not to notice. Oh, she wanted out.

"Don't even think about it, Marcy. If you walk out of here, you will have to go through the front door also."

Her mother's energy seemed to have returned. She straightened up in the chair and waited for her husband to join in.

He looked from his wife to his daughter, and back to his wife.

"Marcy is...?"

"I really don't know," replied Aretha, her look of disgust sweeping down Marcy's middle.

Marcy looked straight before her. Her stillness belied her silent wish that she could conjure up some powerful and benevolent force to eject her from the room: through the roof, the window, the door, the floor. Anywhere. She did not care.

Bradley had been somewhat conscious that his daughter was socializing more these days but was comfortable that it was in their circle. The parents in the circle were also bonded so there was no need to think that there was anything out of place. When he saw her being collected on the weekend in her party clothes, he was unperturbed. He thought his wife was forgetting their own teen escapades. So, with a hectic schedule in his engineering firm, he had paid scant attention. The government had employed him to design some of the roads under construction and that kept him busy.

Aretha looked at him accusingly and pushed her chair to place some distance between them.

"You weren't listening to me. I told you about my concern. I was alone in this. . ."

Her voice broke.

He was scared.

"Marcy is becoming something we did not bargain for. Oh, I can't bear this. This will kill me. I can't imagine any daughter of mine becoming embrangled in situations such as I am hearing about."

She rose and stood before the sink but was soon leaning over and groaning in pain.

She shook off Bradley's offer of comfort and flounced out of the kitchen, leaving her expensive glasses on the table. That was something she never did.

Things went downhill from that point, and the heteroclite threesome found living together unbearable. Quarrels were frequent and Marcy became even more open with her actions. It was as though she was daring her parents to stop her from carrying on the loathsome relationship. It seemed to them that she was no longer waiting for university. She was losing herself in the mire of a relationship with someone who could not measure up.

"Marcy, your fiancé is a businessman? What business is that?" Aretha forced herself to ask one day as she came onto the front porch where Marcy was working on her computer.

Marcy had become very busy as her mother arrived. She typed rapidly and anxiously peered on the screen, muttering unintelligible sounds. Her mother apparently had not noticed.

"Mom, he is not my fiancé, and he is doing good business marketing." She tried the causal tone.

"Marketing what? He does not look professional."

Marcy knew where this could go.

At other times, it was her father.

"So, you say this fellow lives in Ballin Meadows? There is a Ballin Meadows? How close is that to Ballin Pen? What kind of place is that?" He had come outside, briefcase in hand, as she watered the plants on either side of the driveway and had paused from his usual brisk walk to question her before getting into the car.

She kept the hose going, determined not to be drawn into an argument. They were just too ugly. And while she was in their house, she did not want to be rude.

Her relationship with Hughie grew stronger as the relationship with her parents weakened. Hughie offered a respite from the turbulent home situation. She became resentful of the abstemious order of the household. She had been cultured into rising early, doing chores, going to school, returning within deadlines to do homework, other chores and go to bed. On the weekends she met friends who were all of the same order and bored and adventurous. But when she told them of her plans, they were all dubious although she impressed on them how desperate she was.

However, they were not aware that her move was imminent, or someone would have warned her parents. Her misgivings started on the very day she walked into the house at Ballin Meadows. It was a new phase of the action. The taxi took her along the somewhat familiar streets to the one-bedroom flat she had not minded before. But on opening the door to the living room, she was struck by the fact that this was now home. In sudden confusion, she had rested her suitcase on the linoleum-covered floor and sat on the couch from where she took a detailed look.

This is home? she asked herself. Yes, it is, she responded to herself, it is.

She awakened to the sound of someone shuffling in the otherwise silent room. The grogginess fled involuntarily, and her mind jumped into sharp focus. She wished she had stayed asleep. The truth was that he did not deliberately awaken her when he returned at nights. It was just that he was not as quiet as he thought, and she was inevitably aroused. Usually, there was so much movement that it seemed as if some very complex activities were in progress. And each bore a sound so recognizable and ordered that she could wordlessly enact the entire scene which he played out every time he returned in the dead of the night.

"So, you don't know who you living with?" was Marion's incredulous query.

"No. I knew there was something out of place, but I was just waiting. We promised to tell each other the truth at all times."

"Ha! Ha! What? You so foolish. Wake up girl," she said, rolling her eyes in disbelief. "You not ready," she concluded as she wheeled through the gate. "Ba-a-ay!" she jeered, her tongue sticking out.

That was a very sobering conversation for Marcy. She wished she had met Marion before.

But Marion was not the type of girl that she would find in her world. Her circle was the home of middle class, high school or young professional girls and boys. There were trysts, but the incidents of crime among the group were almost nonexistent. Yes, there were instances when girls stepped outside of their boundaries. And there were many things that they engaged in that belied the disciplined and law abiding front. But there was no loose bosom, bleached-out skin Marion with the thick stockings in the heat and the ridiculously long eyelashes and the long, blonde false hair that was now stringy and falling apart.

This was life in a different colour. Her reaction to her first experience with a street dance hall video was a frequent joke in her new social circle.

"You should see the eyes," Marion said, demonstrating her expression. "They nearly pop out."

And indeed, she did not expect such a large, growing gathering. Men and women and boys and girls of all ages converged on a space adjoining a shop. There was even a young man in a wheelchair. He shook his body and moved his only able limbs up and down with vigour, as though he were exercising. She learnt that he had lost both legs in a drive-by shooting. But it was the video stars that got her. A young girl of about seventeen, dressed in a two-piece bikini-style outfit, was "dancing" with a shirtless young man of about the same age. They were so explicit in their moves that she turned her face away many times. Finally, she quietly withdrew.

It had taken her months after she had started living with Hughie to grasp the significance of his frequent night trips, the many times he was away for the whole night, the unacknowledged calls on his phone and very often the discreet meetings with friends. Sometimes, she caught a few words of the telephone conversations which made her numb inside. She had not told anyone of her experience because there was no one to tell. Not her parents who had vowed to distance themselves from her if she became a cohort of someone they hardly knew and who did not seem to have any solid income-earning activity.

She was always mentally unprepared when he came home in the nights. She cringed at the scrape of a drawer being pulled out and the thud of an object being thrown in almost carelessly. That drawer was closed and locked and as on other such occasions, a jingle indicated that the key was removed. Her tortured mind followed the sound of another drawer being opened and the unmistakable muffled sounds in the wardrobe. A bundle of clothes was dumped on the bed, its weight straining the sheet with which she covered. She realized that her involuntary gasp was loud enough for him to hear because he gave an unexpected intake of breath and hesitated in his steps. But then he continued walking as if to say, he was accustomed to those reactions.

For a long time after this, time was defined by the long pulsating silence. Then there was the continuous shuffling around the room ... and there was her waiting. She wished she could sleep but she was no good at pretending and he already knew she was awake and that she would not fall asleep as soon as he came. He knew her mind was busy flitting over events, scenes, words that she could not interpret and that he would not interpret for her.

"Damn gal," he swore softly to himself. "Dem wah rule man, like big man a bwoy. She caa satisfy — look how much money a bring. Right now, a come home wid a big box a Kentucky and the biggest bottle a drinks a could fine. She lucky! Nuff man like me nah do dat. She better shut her trap!" However, if anyone asked him what he was fuming about, he would not have been able to tell.

Through carefully shielded eyes, she saw him walk in the glow of the night light to the bathroom door. He turned briefly, casting what seemed like a careless glance at her. She squeezed her eyes closed. He turned to go, but not before she had seen his eyes narrow. She saw the door close and her stomach relaxed. She pulled the covers further under her neck, wishing they could somehow make her invisible.

Without a word, he sauntered into the bathroom. She knew his mood was changing. For some unknown reason, he went to the wash basin before the shower, and he always did — so funny. While the water ran continuously, she tried to relax her numbed mind. She tried focusing on the furious beating of the water on the tiled floor of the shower; oh, she tried, until her mind felt strained and dazed. As the water pounded, she grew more tense, expecting its cessation any minute. It was a time of torture for her soul. Always, she wished she could just watch television and enjoy the programme. She wanted to be able to pretend that they were just an ordinary couple. Heavens, she tried. But her overactive mind would not let her.

She had tried for the eleven months they had been living together to obliterate the fear of what he might be engaged in — after all, she reasoned, she had no evidence. She had seen nothing. Yes, she had heard the veiled comments of neighbours who seemed to want her to be aware of some truth or other. Perhaps, out of caution, nobody was explicit, at least not verbally. But the meaning was clear. Was it her suspicious mind or was it true that there was a hidden coldness beneath his engaging manner? Did she once or twice, feel some discomfort as if there was some lurking danger?

The water stopped. The smell of soap on his freshly washed body drifted ahead of him into the bedroom. She always found the smell of his bath soap too pungent and was glad when it wore off a little. She would remind herself to buy him the one she preferred. For a moment, she was overcome with terror as his weight bore down on the edge of the bed. She pulled her breath in so sharply that it hurt her chest. The moment hung. . . then the weight of his body pressed the mattress down and the comforter removed after what seemed like several minutes. He wanted to cover too. Funny. Even he wanted to shut out the coolness of the night air. She exhaled.

Somehow, lying on her back had become uncomfortable. She turned onto her stomach, resting her head on her hands, her face towards the gold rimmed clock over the dressing table. The minutes passed slowly. She knew she could not endure this living any longer.

She could run as someone dared to suggest — it would have to be very far. She searched furtively for options, but each led to a huge obstacle. She was caught in a web of indecision and uncertainties, the solutions like spirits evading her every time she came close.

By the time the door opened, she had prepared her mind for the inevitable. She felt his hesitation at the foot of the bed. Through the corner of her eye, she saw that he noted her change in position — a cynical smile playing momentarily about his hard mouth. Like a caged animal, he moved closer, dropping his clothes and towel in a heap on the floor. Caught in the glow of the night light, his long face was grim, his eyes fierce with some unrecognised emotion. She averted her eyes from the tough muscles of his body, an almost unbearable tension rising in her chest and throat.

But he was in a strange mood. Apart from what was obviously meant to be a fond squeeze on the shoulder, he said nothing else to her. He seemed very thoughtful tonight. She was not sure what this was about and instead of feeling restful, she felt tension rise again inside her. Had he heard something? Did one of her friends blab her mouth? She always felt she should not share some privacies with a particular member of the group but generally they were so strongly bonded. They did everything together. They shared their dreams and fears. They all had visions of a better life. They shared laughter and pain. They went on outings with the children and by themselves. Dassa and Lorna had two children each, but she had none. They thought she was very fortunate to have no one to worry about if she needed to make a move. Making a move was a common theme of their conversations — generally it expressed an intention to make a bold change such as get a job or change the area of residence. But at times it referred to a vague plan to leave the life. The latter would only be shared with the inner core of confidantes, of which there were two. Her inertia and theirs was not born out of what her mother called worthlessness. It was really out of a deep fear of failing as she had done twice before.

The last time, she had left home to go to the market with an oversized bag. Fear was a very common feeling. She would never forget the feeling of utter panic that overtook her as she disembarked from the taxi and came almost face to face with a neighbour who lived in the lane. Sandy was an area girl born and bred. She knew no other life except the life behind the zinc fence, the frolicking Fridays, the endless round of streetside hair stylists, makers of dancehall clothes, the soup, crab and corn on the corner. A world that was previously unknown to Marcy. Trembling, she had swiftly turned into the market. She had cursed softly as she blamed herself for not being more alert — she had forgotten she was on the run and not yet free. That evening she walked nervously home from the bus stop, hoping that Sandy was not anywhere nearby to remind her of the incident. In great despondency, she unpacked the groceries and in mere tokenism, fixed the usual meal.

Her heart was heavy, and she felt uncaring of what the meal turned out to be. Such was her despondency. Her thoughts were as still as a pool of stagnant water. In automaton-like fashion, she rinsed and dried the pots, and placed them on the two-burner gas stove which she listlessly lit. While she was comfortable with the nice furnishings in the other areas of the house, she hated the kitchen. It was pathetically basic and so she spent little time there. She always wondered what her mother would say if she saw her in a kitchen like this.

She was so engrossed in her misery that she had only noticed the faint smell of gas after she had struck the match. In seconds, the room became a huge blazing boom. She felt her body growing more numb with each passing second but she did not have the will to redirect her thoughts. The mesmeric effect of the dancing reddish-yellow flame lulled her into a state akin to drunkenness and she could think of nothing that was rational. Then the kitchen seemed to burst into angry flames, so high that anyone outside could see them as they leaped threateningly in the direction of the ceiling. The kitchen became so smoky she could not see anything clearly. Everything was an etching, an abstract item lying in a dark, white cloud that was now swirling crazily around. At last, she summoned her previously immobilized body to move but the dulling effect of the smoke was too much.

After a while, her lungs began to feel choked up and she started coughing loud, racking coughs, but they were contained in her grey, smoky space and would not be heard. She was overcome by listlessness and drowsiness, and her coughs became terribly painful sounds.

She woke painfully and slowly to a blur of voices which seemed far away. As she journeyed back to consciousness, she realized that she was in a room which smelled of antiseptic. It was quiet except for the voices. She could not find the energy to open her eyes, but someone noticed that she had moved and made an alarm. Drowsily, she lay there while they talked persuasively to her, but her eyes could not respond, and she gave up. Her mouth felt dry and crisp. Her hands felt as though they were carrying weights. And her stomach hurt badly. She struggled in an abyss of almost unbearable pain, where voices she could not quite interpret dropped unclear thoughts into her mind. In that lack of definition of place, time and events, she had no crutch. The next few days passed in a blur, and only briefly and occasionally did she know where she was or who was around her. And when she did, the muscles of her mouth just refused to flex, causing her to retreat into the unreal world.

She awoke to see him standing over her, a look of deep concern on his face. Her neighbours, Sandra and Marion, greeted her and expressed pleasure at being there when she came to, and after a few moments politely walked out of the room. Her dazed mind could not quite comprehend her circumstances but there was a negative reaction to him. When he bent to peck her on the cheek, she felt her heartbeat quicken and her breath became sharp, and she wanted to scream but could not. There was a wall of tension between them. He tried to offer comfort but felt her unspoken rejection.

He left, realizing that he could not penetrate her consciousness. "Good thing I came home early today." He breathed hard, thinking of what might have happened. "I will come back tomorrow. Hope you can talk." He pointed to the bag he had brought and walked in deep thought towards the door.

Those were his last words to her. She did not hear of the incident in which he was shot and crippled until a week after it happened. And when she heard, she was filled with such a depth of sadness that she cried huge, wracking, painful sobs for his life and hers, forever changed, and for the lives of their friends who were positioned to experience a similar fate.

Too Late

"Wooooy!" Carl shouted as he jammed bottles of liquor into the cartons arranged near the door of the bar. He had already taken all of the unopened boxes from the storeroom and was cruising now, having exceeded the quota set by his team. Even in the dim light he could see that there were hundreds of them, and he wanted them all — well, not all for himself, he thought good naturedly, because Dave and Jimmy were not covering outside for nothing.

The steady patter of the raindrops was reassuring. Carl was certain that most people would have to be dragged out on a night like this. But he had been well geared up. In addition to the dark coloured pants, he wore a thick black sweater and a black knitted hat pulled well over his ears. Carl, a huge twenty-four year old, had the appearance of a hulk but he moved as swiftly and as deftly as a panther. For months he had been doing this and almost always afterwards there was the feeling of dissatisfaction, of regret. But it seemed that every time someone told him of a 'gold mine' he was stone broke, thus his resolution not to return never lasted. The few dollars he earned from selling snacks and cigarettes could not go far — certainly not as far as his baby mother and children. Remembering

Pauline's annoyance with him the last time he took her the maintenance money brought him back into sharp focus.

"Where you going with that?" she had demanded. If she were not so diminutive, her threatening tone would have scared him. "You better take it and..." she screamed at him in that hateful rasping voice that at times caused him to lose his temper.

In helpless anger he had retaliated, "I giving you all I have! What the hell you want me to do?"

In response she had whirled into the house and flung at him from inside, "Stay there let me tell you what to do to mine you own pickney dem." He knew the barrage of missiles that would follow and had quietly withdrawn from the scene ... in fear of himself and in fear of her.

There was no time to assess the value of the goods, but he was sure it was quite a haul and although this mission had not been his brainchild, he felt honoured to be playing such a central role. He worked steadily, his attuned ears registering only the clink of his bottles inside, and outside, the soft comforting sound of the rain and seemingly distant barking of the dogs in the residences. Very infrequently there was the lonely sound of a vehicle which quickly faded into the distance of the night. Striking at midnight was not just a badge of distinction for the team; it was also for them a time when most people would be off the streets and as long as they were obtrusive with their actions, they would most likely be undetected.

Every time a box was filled, he rapped on the door and this was answered by a single rap from outside. Then Dave made his brief and well-timed appearance in the doorway, and promptly collected the box. Everything had been skilfully choreographed. Jimmy would continue to cover while Dave relayed the boxes to the hiding place. He relied on Dave to select the rest of the players, all of whom had to be of the highest quality — able to keep their mouths shut, fearless and teachable. His movements were swift and sure. He had been inside this bar several times and he knew where the best loot was. God, he thought, after all this he deserved a bottle of the best scotch but that would have been an unforgiveable action.

His pacing became fast and fierce, and goaded by purpose. He was driven by the need to succeed, to make this heist the most rewarding. He wanted to earn enough to address some urgent matters. There had been times when he had wanted to live a more normal life, going to work and getting paid at the end of a week or month, buying a house in a quiet area, getting married and rearing children whom he could really take care of. Like many young people, he had this vision.

Had serendipity been positive or negative? What if he had not been socializing with his friend at the bar near his home one Friday evening and had not been introduced to someone who could help him to find a job? What if he had known the nature of the job or had not pursued the offer? What if he did not have the children ever wanting and the mother — Jesus, the mother! After two years of the worst nagging anyone had ever endured, he had moved out one night after a relentless bout of cursing, her words flying all over the place like bullets fired by an unskilled hand. Only, these were connecting and hurting his very soul.

His introduction to this livelihood was routine. As a neophyte for the first three months, he was only given less risky jobs such as surveillance or checking areas before the occasion. But his skill was soon recognized, and he became fully integrated into the operations of the group. It was at that point he was offered a gun, which he refused. He also did not like the trite treatment of killing someone as displayed by the leader of the gang.

"We don't want no nappy wearer goin' out with us," the serious-faced, business-like leader had declared emphatically one evening. This was while they sat at a planning session at a restaurant, one of several places they had carefully chosen for their meetings. The other four men laughed sardonically as though on cue.

"Mummy will shelter you," one said. He raised his glass, inviting the others to follow. To his surprise, two did not follow but continued their own jesting. "This is no business for fools," the leader continued, looking piercingly at Carl. "We have to be ready to defend. This is a career."

At that Carl laughed and said, "Man, you think this is a career?"

"You think this is bank work?" the leader countered. "Go behind the counter, teller," he said sarcastically.

To avoid further disagreements he had quietly extricated himself and knowing fully well that that could have been dangerous, he relocated to another city where he could lose himself. But he was still in need of an income and despite a valiant effort at finding a job that was above board, he did not succeed. The old life beckoned. So, he found another gang, a very benign group it seemed at first. He had become so comfortable that when the gun issue arose again, he decided to just sidestep it. He did that for several months.

He was just about to rap on the door when he heard a sharp, low whistle, but not as low as they had planned. And just then he had the horrifying thought that there might have been others. Saviour divine, he had to get out. Dave and Jimmy were probably miles away by now. His body tensed and in an involuntary movement he touched his pocket, feeling for the hardness there. He recalled that he had first refused to carry the gun he had been offered. In fact, he discouraged the use of guns. He did not want to hurt anyone, not he. He just wanted some money. He had broken up with one team because the leader had insisted on arming all the men, but not Carl. No gun for him, he had insisted. He preferred to depend on his adroitness.

Listening carefully, he eased himself out through the back door of the bar, the lock of which they had prised open earlier. He was thankful for the cover of trees, the drizzling rain, and the darkness. He could only make out the shiny zinc roofs of the nearby shops, all of which had their backs on the gully. The two lights that would have provided visibility had been broken days before in anticipation of the operation. They thought they had covered every possibility. They almost felt safe.

Peering into the darkness and discerning no threatening presence, he quickly slipped behind a tree, his back to the gully and giving himself a chance to get accustomed to the darkness, he focused on the front of the compound. The drizzle, which was getting heavier by the minute, played havoc with his vision, making him very uneasy. After a while he could hear what sounded like voices and he eased the hat from his ears and strained to distinguish the sounds which were obviously carefully kept low. Then there were unmistakable footsteps stealthily coming closer and sometimes briefly hesitating as though uncertain. Sometimes there was no sound at all and at other times they would seem to be near him, to the left, to the right ... he was confused. He could not move if he was uncertain. That could be suicidal.

For a fleeting moment he thought about Dave and Jimmy and the get together they would soon be having. Man, it would be a celebration. Plenty of partying. Lots of juice because they would be getting a good price. His face relaxed into a smile as he dreamed about the children's clothes and food, and about the mother's softening attitude towards him. Money is magic, he thought. It opens doors for you. As he mused, he suddenly realised that there was a dead quiet. Even the rain had ceased. It was like the stillness of an empty churchyard on a Sunday night. He dared not move. After long seconds he could hear those steps again. And still he could not tell where they were coming from, where they were going or how many there were. He was afraid for the first time, and wished that he had the benefit of the added obstacle of the falling rain. The tension became unbearable. He could not be sure of anything except the gnawing feeling that he might be in real danger. It was a fear he had never felt before on any of these raids.

As if on cue from his mind, he shifted his position mechanically and unfortunately stepped on what felt and sounded like an empty drink box. He exhaled in horror. The ensuing crunch seemed to hang for seconds... his heart was pumping hard, and he gritted his teeth in anticipation. Then he could hear the footsteps, loud and deliberate... running... running. Carl tried hard to clear his dazed thoughts. There seemed to be a hundred men moving between the trees. Too late, he realised he should have jumped the gully from the start. Too late...

Carl felt the muscles of his face go rigid. His palms grew moist and clammy as he clenched and unclenched his hands. His throat was dry, and he was breathing like a fish that had been thrown on dry land. With shaking hands, he pulled the gun from under his shirt, although his blurred mind could not have fathomed a reason if he were asked why. It was as instinctual as the snake's response to a threatening presence that he might have sensed rather than seen. His partners would laugh at him if they could see him now.

"When I use my brain, I feel better," he had said over and over. Sitting at a table of cards and bottles of beer one night, he had responded to their teasing in his usual calm manner.

"You think is brains dem man use," Dave had quipped, not raising his eyes from his hand.

"Boy, I would never kill a man," Carl said, his voice strong with conviction.

"But a man will," said Jimmy, pausing emphatically, "kill you."

"Well, they have to catch me first," Carl responded, obviously resolving not to allow that to happen.

Jimmy had laughed in disbelief, asking whether he thought these missions were picnics. But Carl took great pride in outsmarting the police.

On another occasion when he and his friends had robbed another bar on the other side of the gully, the loot had been sent safely off when he heard a siren. Although he was not sure that there was any connection to his situation, he had taken immediate precaution to change into a suit of clothing that looked like an old man's, complete with hat and walking stick, and had safely passed the radio car on the nearby corner. Afterwards, he related the drama to the others amidst uproarious laughter. On other occasions, the lawmen arrived late on the scene and did not have any leads to follow. So, he had had good reason to be comfortable with the security system they had set up. But tonight, he was not so sure.

Like foxes, his hunters came in the blanket of darkness, their steps light and purposeful. Carl was rooted to his position behind the tree. Then someone shouted, "Hey partner, I smell him", and another eagerly replied, "Thief, weh yuh deh?", and the darkness came alive with running footsteps.

"Where's the bastard?" someone else asked close by and Carl was face to face with a policeman. The officer's long-range gun was pointing slightly sideways as he had apparently been about to go in that direction. There was a flicker of surprise in the officer's eyes, a flicker of fear in Carl's and for a few moments nobody moved. Then as if remembering his mission, the policeman moved forward, simultaneously aligning his weapon with his quarry. In that split second, Carl, as though drugged, had raised his gun and pulled the trigger. The policeman jumped aside and fell, giving him a chance to run. There followed a confusion of shouting voices, blaring sirens and the flashing of blue lights, urging him to make good his escape. In the melee which followed, he dropped the gun, his unwelcome companion.

"Got him?" a voice asked in expectation and Carl did not hesitate. He was running with one thought in mind. He must get to the gully. He must reach the part where there was no meshed fence. As the huge cavern opened up before him, an angry voice said, "Get that dirty killer!"

This was followed by a volley of curses, punctuated by clearly distinguishable sounds of gunshots that seemed to be aimed in different directions. It was as though they were ensuring that the whole area was swept. The shrill, terrifying blast of the whistle sent him on a wild dash to the edge of the gully. He hesitated briefly. The light-coloured flooring of the gully along with the rays of lights on the other side lightened the darkness somewhat. But understanding his limited options, in a sudden orchestrated movement, he dropped flat onto his belly and holding on to the edge, he swung his legs over and found a foothold on the side. This allowed him to stand gripping the edge with his face towards the bar. Trembling, he quickly rehearsed his next move. He did not need to hear the boots of his pursuers resolutely pounding the wet earth, nor the urgent wailing of the sirens growing louder outside on the street.

By the time the policemen had reached the edge, he had coldly calculated his next move. When the angry voice shouted "Halt!", he had quickly arched his back outwards and jumped the twenty or so feet below, landing with a painful jolt. Momentarily, he felt unbalanced, his insides feeling as though they had been placed in a container and stirred vigorously around. He dared not breathe. It's over, he thought as the shots pierced the wall of rain and haze. They are going to get me. Dave and Jimmy, he screamed inside, where are you? The rain was pouring now, making it difficult for him to see. The voices of his pursuers became muffled. The occasional nature of the gunshots told him that even with their powerful flashlights, the pursuers could not see him clearly. He tried to steady himself, regain his balance. As he limped forward, a shot whizzed past his head, causing him to forget his pain. Soon he had recovered enough to go faster, and he was running in a zig-zag fashion down the gully, keeping as close to the side as he could.

It was agony. The dirty water underfoot splashed his clothes and many times he stepped into something soft and squishy. He did not want to know what it was, and he could not escape the stench. The place reeked of filth, rubbish and dead animals but this did not matter if he could just reach where the road crossed the gully. There was a little settlement there into which the police did not care to follow anyone because of the circuitous routes which they did not understand. He had to get there. Four more minutes of hard running would get him there. Thankfully, the water was flowing towards the centre of the gully so that was no impediment.

On and on he ran, all the time trying to maintain his grip on the wet and slippery concrete. The rain was easing up, making his passage easier. On and on he ran, not mindful of the soreness of his muscles or drenched clothes which stuck to his body like a skin. At long last he saw the road. He started breathing easier, but he did not slow. He was going to make it. He had shaken them off. He was panting hard now. His legs felt as though they would give way. Not now, he urged mentally. In rhythmic tones his mind kept energizing him. *Have to get there. Must get there.* Then at last he was there. Like the proverbial long-distance runner, he made one last lunge that took him right under the bridge on which the road sat.

He looked joyfully at the steep little path, now slippery from the rain, that would take him up to the road. From there he would cross over to the other side of the bridge and quickly walk the three or four chains to the entrance of the scheme. He knew that once inside he need not worry. He would rest with his friend who was always willing to bail him out. It felt good to know this. The tightness in his chest evaporated and he stooped, head down, to rest for a few seconds. Just one more hurdle — at long last to get unnoticed across the bridge and into the scheme. The rest was easy. Every now and then he glanced at the bridge to make sure. "Wow!" he said to himself. That was damn close. He did not want to allow thoughts of the policeman whom he might have hit. He prayed that he had not been killed. He was just defending himself. Which man didn't do that?

Relief mixed with regret as he raised his head and turned towards the path. He would make that last effort, and in a moment, he would ascend to the road. With his last reserve of energy, he moved from under the bridge and towards the steps in the slope leading up to the road. But just before he lifted his leg to place it on the first step, there was a sudden sense of a presence nearby, an uncomfortable and inexplicable feeling of being observed. For a moment, only a moment, he hesitated in uncertainty and then he raised his head upwards towards the road.

He staggered as though entranced. Two shadowy figures stood on the bridge with faces turned in the direction of the gully. He did not need to see them clearly. He knew who they were. He slowly and pointedly held his hands up and having received the reassurance required, lowered them to grip the slippery slope as he ascended to the road.

A World Apart

Eric sat at the back of the class musing on the different happenings in the front. He enjoyed the distant low buzz of voices as his classmates anxiously attacked the assignment given that morning. His eyes brooded and his pencil dangled leisurely over the page as he waited for inspiration to make the first mark. The soft chatter of voices soothed him, and he felt comfortable in his belief that the teacher would not be able to reach him by the end of the class. Most times it was like that, but he did not mind. He did not mind when she started at the front and slowly worked her way towards the back.

"Joshua, this is incorrect," she had just said sternly to the classmate they called Square Head, and she proceeded to show him how to solve the long division problem.

"You must carry this over. Now this becomes thirty and not just zero. So now you divide thirty by ten. Do you understand?" she asked after her painstaking explanation.

To Eric's amusement, the hypocrite answered, "Yes, Miss." And from his busy appearance after the teacher's personal attention, anyone would have thought that he was working through the ten problems.

Eric could have given Miss Briggs a medal for taking that route through the class and another for keeping it that way until the end of the year when he would be off for summer holidays. Class was a comfortable din of whispers and low-toned sounds, and sometimes a louder than allowed giggle surfaced. But in general, it was a world he did not understand so he went to great pains to look at it from the outside. When many of his classmates proudly displayed ticks at the end of the class as they compared notes, Eric could never show his book because there was very little beyond starts in them. And although he thought about it sometimes, he could never completely understand why.

On this day, Eric did try to work out the problem, but he could not figure out all the elements of long division. He would be in trouble again if Miss Briggs managed to reach him this time because she had called earlier for anyone who did not understand to come to the table. So, he sat there feeling as if he was standing behind the fence of a racetrack and as the horses galloped past he was trying to follow a specific one but gave up as it disappeared into the fray of pounding feet, whips and dust.

He knew Miss Briggs had been frustrated with his below average performance for the entire year. But although he should be trying his hardest to understand everything in preparation for the end of year examinations, he just could not concentrate.

His best friends, Kevin and Jake, had passed the Grade 6 examination a year ago and had moved on to the high school seven miles away. The high point of his week, every week, was Saturday, when he met with them at the youth club. His eyes rolled when he heard of their new exploits.

"Eric, our friend Jake get plenty lunch money, so almost every day him at the Chiney restaurant eating," Kevin said one day as they sat on the steps of the community centre waiting for the president to come.

"No, man," said Jake. "I do chores for my neighbour and get paid every week, but I don't spend it. I save it, so that's how I can buy a nice lunch."

"Man, Eric, Anglin Town not like Salem. It have hospital, pretty shops, a big library and many, many cars. Cars like dirt. It's a busy place. You must come with us one day," said Kevin. But he knew that that could not happen during the week.

"Eric. I have a good idea. Study hard and see if you can pass the Grade 6 exam. You can come to City High just like us. You can do it, Eric. We not brighter than you. You just never study," said Jake, not able to hide the longing on his face. "That's why you missed the Common Entrance."

Eric looked with interest at Jake. He hadn't ever thought of that. Jake stood expectantly, looking at his friend. It was as though he was challenging him.

Evidently, the suggestion had sparked Kevin's interest because he suddenly became very animated. His voice pitched high in agreement.

"Ye-e-es, Eric. We will help you. Let's meet every Sunday evening to study."

"But we not doing the same thing," said Eric uncertainly, looking from one to the other.

"No matter," countered Kevin. "We will help one another."

"I will have to tell grandmother," said Eric hesitantly. His interest was piqued but he did not want to give a definite answer.

Eric did not ask his grandmother anything. So, the weeks passed and the boys met but as boys were, there was no pressure on Eric.

"Eric." He heard her beside him, her piercing, irritating voice breaking him out of his reverie. No matter how she pitched her voice, it was so jarring that he wanted to shut it out. She was at his desk. He did not raise his eyes above the dark skirt and long-sleeved sheer pink blouse with the pink cardigan over it. And he tried not to notice the familiar scent of perfume or lotion that accompanied her everywhere.

"Eric," she said, speaking just for him. "Let me see what you have done."

Eric shifted the book grudgingly to the side of his desk so that she could see the answers he had arrived at, or rather, his effort to solve the problems. He kept his eyes lowered, waiting for the exclamation and the rebuke. He was conscious of the penetrating eyes of his classmates as they strained to hear every word Miss Briggs uttered. The class was as still as a house asleep at night. The waiting stretched and strained. Eric fidgeted. The teacher looked wordlessly at the book. Eric wanted to see her face but dared not look up. He dared not turn lest he touched her. He was as stiff as a piece of pine board.

And then Eric reacted. Let her stand there, he thought, for the rest of the class. Let me see how long she can last. Let them all wait for the eruption. It won't bother me. And he started to feel energy flowing back into his body as his mind felt easier and easier. His shoulder returned to a resting state and his breathing normalized.

Then Miss Briggs moved. She reached for the book as though knowing what she would see and held it in her hand. He could feel her go taut. He could hear her breathing as though she was running uphill. Eric felt his chest tightening and he could not help glancing at her. Her face bore that tight, strained look. Her red-painted mouth was as puckered as a rose and she moved her pen nib pointing out, across the page and down, clearly not intending to make any mark.

Eric was as nervous as a leaf in rough wind. I could go to the bathroom now, he thought. I could. I have to move now. The storm will break any minute.

"Teacher, can I go outside?" he asked quietly, the words squeezed out through barely opened teeth, his eyes fixed on the desk before him.

There was no answer.

"Teacher, I need to go to the bathroom," he said, shifting the desk just a little. The sounds he made, meant to have been inaudible, seemed to have attracted the attention of the curious class, for his tentative glance showed that all actions seemed to have been arrested and everyone had a look of disguised alertness.

Miss Briggs momentarily shifted her eyes from the page that she seemed to have found curiously fascinating, to Eric who had abruptly pushed his chair a fraction of an inch further from the desk.

"Come with me, Eric," she invited in mock entreaty, turning with book in hand, towards the passage leading to the front of the room and expectedly to her desk.

Eric jumped to his feet, sending the desk bumping into the chair before him and almost sending his neighbour crashing to the floor. His consciousness of the inevitability of the attention evoked by the scene aroused his shame and his annoyance.

"I want to pee!" he shouted, moving swiftly towards the door. "To pee is what I want now," he hurled at her, scuttling towards the door.

"Pee Eric? Pee, Eric?" asked Miss Briggs. "Go, Eric. Go pee," she ended, her voice providing the melody to the loud crescendo of laughter in the background.

Like a scared puppy, Eric ran to the back of the yard behind the row of bathrooms, not knowing where else to go. From there he could hear the distant mingling of sounds from the classes, sometimes the ongoing buzz being interrupted by a conspicuous peal of laughter, a shout or a scream. His hiding place was quiet enough for now but he knew he had to escape before the bell rang.

He had to get away and the only route would be through the gate which was at the front of the yard and visible from the principal's office. He would not arouse any suspicion passing the block of classrooms that was parallel to his block — children had to go outside at times. However, they were not allowed through the gate during class times.

But he would have to try.

The windows of the office were wide open and from what he could see, the principal was not inside. He stealthily moved towards the gate some yards from the office and staffroom.

His grandmother's words, "When you salt, you salt", echoed in his ears when Miss Brigg's voice penetrated his benumbed mind.

"Eric Mair, you finish peeing. Where are you going, sir?" Miss Briggs was just approaching the corner of the block to pass the staffroom. From there she would enter the door between it and the principal's office.

Eric froze. He looked straight ahead, seeing only the wall. She was beside him now, wearing a suspicious looking smile. "So, you were coming back to class, weren't you? Or were you going elsewhere?" She was now holding his upper arm and pulling him towards the class. He could not bear it. But he could not pull against the teacher.

As soon as Miss Briggs stepped in with her cargo, the giggling started and was threatening to explode again but the class knew her, so they giggled hesitantly.

"I want to hear no more of the raucous laughter in this room. Eric has finished his 'activity'," she paused, "and is now ready for some hard work."

She dropped her face in emphasis and turned her back to him while eyeing him from over her shoulder. The giggling became a diminuendo that had to be contented with clandestine nudges and facial expressions while work continued.

"Sit right here, Eric," said Miss Briggs. "Peeing time is over and now it's math time."

Eric thought she deliberately kept her voice high enough to be heard by the front rows. She showed no awareness that she was rewarded by their struggle to control the bubbling laughter.

Eric felt subdued. He allowed her calm but firm voice to penetrate his consciousness. He realized that the class was no longer poised for mocking him and he started breathing easily, no longer a hundred-meter runner. He reached into his pencil case and retrieved his sharpest pencil.

When Miss Briggs had marked out a square of the blackboard with bright red chalk, she came close to him, bent, and whispered,

"No more peeing."

"No, Miss," Eric answered as a wave of understanding gently approached and washed over his troubled spirit. Excitement welled up inside, so strong, he was afraid it would gush out somewhere in front of him.

The few giggles showed that her last admonition had not escaped everybody but he felt determined, a convert to learning. He was going to do as the teacher said. He would be going to City High School. Kevin and Jake said he could. For the first time, he understood what it took to get to City High School.

Night Mystery

It was nighttime again — a time I feared. Ever since I moved to this house, I had not been able to sleep. I had spent night after night for the past two months in a torment of the worst sort. I had moved here with great anticipation to this cosy, classy, older-type, middle-income home, urban yet detached from the heart of the city. One could relax here I thought, the day I had gone to look at the house. Though obviously old, it was well-kept. The clean beige-coloured walls, the huge round bedrooms and spacious dining room — they do not make them that large anymore — won my heart. And the expansive yard, grassy green, with its proliferation of trees scattered pleasingly over it, and the wildness of the rock garden of green plants, roses, aromatic herbs, pink, red and purple potted bougainvilleas and the like, made up my mind for me. Yes, I would take the small side of the house, I told Mrs Parkes, the engaging, elderly landlady who showed me the place. I would have preferred the flat, which was also unoccupied, but it proved too small for me. In my heart I wanted to feel a sense of seclusion.

What was most appealing was that I could take precious Sheila, my loving, watchful puppy. I could see her gamboling across the green grass, her short, fuzzy tail shaking merrily. I could see her chasing birds and butterflies in futility or managing to grab a ground lizard, if there was any, or a rat that had not been swift at making its escape. Yes, Mrs Parkes loved dogs as long as I was careful with the cleaning up. She had not had one for a long time because she was unable to do the stooping. I took careful note.

"Hope we'll get along," Mrs Parkes said smilingly from her wrinkled light-skinned face, her watery eyes inscrutable from age.

We were just coming from inside the apartment which I would occupy. All things considered, it was comfortable. The bedroom and living room retained the pre-modern character. It was very large and airy with shiny wooden floors. Stepping from this area to the other facilities was like changing worlds. The bathroom had been tiled and featured an oval-shaped bath and a wash basin resting comfortably on a polished wooden cupboard. The kitchen had also been upgraded to one with tiled floors, a marble counter, built-in stove and refrigerator, and a space for dining.

"I'm sure we will," I said.

I looked from her face to the surroundings, noting that the area was occupied by a mix of older type houses with a smattering of more modern ones. As I walked with Mrs Parkes across the front of the house, I thought that these homeowners were certainly proud people. Mrs Parkes' flowers were replicated in the neighbouring yards as far as I could see. It was almost a sort of code consisting of pink, yellow, red and white bougainvillea leaning over the fences. Just outside the fence, there was a trail of neatly cropped less ostentatious Duranta gold. Palms, fan banana trees, fruit trees and many others called attention to themselves.

"My mother was the last person to occupy the apartment."

The glasses she is wearing are really ancient, I thought in amusement. Her small eyes, like two dull beads, searched my face.

"And my husband had taken the decision to leave this earth before that. So that leaves my daughter and me. But she flew the nest..."

I turned my attention towards the windows in the effort to avoid her moment of sadness.

"Mrs Parkes, I rather like how the windows surround the room. Seeing them from outside is so different," I said, catching her attention. I saw that she was pleased.

"My dear, my daughter pressured me to change the old French windows, but I refused to change how they were arranged. 'Mom, these windows are just not in', she kept saying. She is the one who wanted the kitchen and bathroom changes. She insisted that the kitchen should be outfitted with the fridge and stove, but the tenant should take all other furnishings."

Oh, I thought, oh!

And so, I took the house, and the landlady too, who, though obviously not of a malignant character, was decidedly a little irksome at times. She wanted to talk in the mornings when I was in the throes of preparing for work, going from the kitchen to bathroom to outside, doing the many little things that comprised the morning routine.

"Yes, Mrs. P, I heard," I responded to her distressed question. Though I did not pay much attention to her response, I did hear it. "No, Mrs P, they haven't found the man."

"Jesus, help us!" she exclaimed. "They must find him!"

"No, don't be scared. Just remember to keep your grille locked. The police are trying hard," I suggested in a kind, understanding voice. Did I know that? No, but I was hurrying.

Mrs P wanted to talk in the evenings, no matter how tired I said I was. She would follow me to the kitchen and even to the bathroom door to continue a conversation. But I liked her. She was sometimes welcome company. My real problem was my nightly experiences.

When I told my friend at work about the unusual happenings in the house at nights, she told me, "You St. Mary people too superstitious."

But this was more than superstition, I insisted, somewhat disappointed by her lack of understanding. I had not felt fear of this sort since I'd left the country five years ago. The urban setting had little reminders of those days of dark shadows.

Back then I lived in a lane that was only lit occasionally by the light of the moon. It was flanked on both sides by banana and sugar cane farms and walking there was a scary experience, especially if you were alone. Then it would not take too long before the walk became a jog, and the jog became a gasping sprint. Steps that sometimes seemed to belong to someone else echoed frighteningly in a darkness lit only by the peenie wallies or the torch. Now, the torch was the creation of every fearful walker. It was made from an empty soda bottle furnished with the precious kerosene oil into which was immersed one end of a rolled newspaper wick.

Most times, even if you came through the darkness unaided, going back became too frightening a thought. So, you would buy a bottle and get a little oil somewhere, since kerosene was not sold after certain hours. And you would proceed, still hesitantly, but a little less afraid. You had the light, but beyond its sphere was still the unknown, and the outer reaches produced shape after grotesque shape in the trees. You, of course, tried not to look beyond your immediate path, but a furtive glance into the depths of the field was almost an involuntary act.

Sheila slept in the house with me every night — Mrs P did not know, obviously, I thought, or else she would have asked for an explanation of the noises of the night before. I wondered also about the neighbours. Were they disturbed and would they complain? There were other dogs in the area, but they did not regularly create such a rumpus. I suffered unimaginable tension every night when she started her relentless barking. All the time she seemed to have a focus, to be barking at a specific object or person stationed outside the windows to the back of the yard. Sometimes she would get really fierce and move forward as though she saw something that she was ready to lunge at. In her agitation, she moved backwards and forwards, breathing hard and every now and then she turned to face me. At these times, I tried to soothe her, but she soon left me to go back to her normal position. I peered into the semidarkness, wishing that the rays of the streetlights had penetrated the obscurity of the yard better. I was scared as hell about what I might see but drawn nevertheless in fearful fascination, particularly when Sheila's slow-paced regular yapping changed momentum and became a ferocious fast-paced barking. I alternated half-an-hour or so in bed, where I dozed fitfully, with another half-an hour spent in watching outside.

Going to work each morning after that was a hellish experience. My head felt like it had been pounded by a sledgehammer, my eyes were baggy, and my entire body felt drugged and weak. I soon concluded that my work was going to start showing the strain — that I had to leave the house now. In spite of the pressure to act, I tried to let reason prevail. I had only been there for two weeks. I would be losing half a month's rent at this house and would still have to find the new rent. It seemed a true dilemma. But when the barking started again that night, my mind was made up. It was either the money or my sanity.

That night, another dimension was added to my alarm: a distinctly rotten smell pervaded the room for several minutes, then drifted away just as I was getting used to it. And the dog barked more fiercely than ever, seeming to move toward some unseen object on which her attention was riveted. I really wanted her inside, but not so noisy. But, strange enough, I heard no comments from my landlady the next morning, either in protest or in query.

Mrs Parkes greeted me in her usual friendly tone, her expression unequivocal. I watched her eyes as she spoke, surrounded by the fine lines of age, her face sprinkled with tiny dark-brown freckles against the light-brown skin. I could not tell: was she watching me? I shrugged the thought away every time it surfaced. No, she was not. Just my imagination.

Mornings on the weekends were unbelievably quiet. I always felt that I had emerged from some nightmarish stay in a dark hole and could not decide how to deal with the peaceful atmosphere. It was as though my true reality was the horror of the nights and the hangover caused a tension that was not easy to shake off. Work days were better because the mornings were so filled with activities, there was no option but to focus on them. But on weekends the fear of the previous night lingered around the house in everything I did: as I cleaned, cooked, washed or swept the yard, it just stayed there, an almost discernible, breathing thing.

I was glad to see my neighbour in her yard this morning, and so I watered my potted plants in a carefully leisurely manner, hoping she would draw near. Our interaction so far had been little more than the cursory polite greeting. An elderly woman, probably a retiree, she usually seemed quite busy doing little things outside —

puttering in the garden, instructing her helper or gardener about cleaning the yard, or sweeping daintily at the film of dirt left on the paved walkway by the gardener.

I hedged around, mulching the pots, tearing off dried leaves and doing other trivial things, hoping she would take notice of me. It worked. Either she sensed my purpose, or her outdoor plans coincided with mine, because after about ten minutes she drifted over towards the fence, where I was now pulling weeds from a large pot of ferns I had placed into the corner. I could not hide my satisfaction. I straightened up and advanced towards where she stood, before a narrow clearing in the hibiscus hedge, a small spade hanging from her right hand, which was folded across her waist, the other arm bent and anchoring it while resting patiently on her hip.

Now that we were so close, I was hesitant about crossing the line. But on the other hand, I desperately wanted to know about the history of the place. She sensed that this was not the usual greeting, that there was something pending, and she gave me a slight, somewhat quizzical smile.

"How's the gardening?" I asked, approaching her, and looking in appreciation at the array of flowers. For a while the sight of the many-coloured blooms, the fluttering butterflies and the smell of the roses held my attention. I became lost in a blur of sensations so powerful I had to wrench my attention away. She was still smiling.

"Oh, I wish my gardener would pay my poor plants some attention," she said, pulling her arms and gesturing with the spade.

Not wanting to downplay her dissatisfaction, I said carefully, "I like your garden. It reminds me of my mother's in the country."

"Thank you. I'm sure your mother takes good care of her garden. I can see that it has rubbed off on you."

"Oh, she does, tirelessly," I said. "Have you lived here very long?" I hurried on, feeling encouraged.

"Oh, yes. I am a long-standing citizen, same as Mrs Parkes. When I came she was already here with her mother, husband and children. Now the poor lady is alone. Well! You are her company now." She said this as though she had heard something.

"Yes?" I said, trying not to show my eagerness.

"This was a quiet place then, when everybody knew everybody else. Life was just nice and calm."

"But it still seems so."

"No, you wouldn't know, my dear. Some of the characters in this once nice neighbourhood..." She shook her head in disbelief.

"Okay?" But she would not move on, and I could not find a way to continue the conversation without seeming deliberate. Losing interest, I said goodbye.

Mechanically, I went through the motions of packing and moving. I thought I would have left the house in profound relief, that I would have happily shaken the dust from my feet, but instead I drove away with a feeling that lacked definition: a little lost, still curious, somewhat regretful.

As though sensing my deep regret, the driver paused outside the gate, allowing me to take a final look at the house.

In the young night light, it just stood there drowsy and implacable. How innocent it looked with its...well... its history. The fence was low enough for the structure to be seen from the roof to the ground garden where the flowers blurred into one sleepy mass, bordered by the well-shaven green yard. It all seemed so unreal now.

It was all against me, mocking me for leaving. It was as though it was saying, "Stupid, it was all in the imagination."

Perhaps, I should ask it to explain my experience.

As I escaped, I shed the fear of the nights before, and embraced the oncoming experience with the flutter of hope in my heart.

www.ingramcontent.com/pod-product-compliance
Ingram Content Group UK Ltd.
Pitfield, Milton Keynes, MK11 3LW, UK
UKHW040032200726
13854UKWH00001B/483